# DEATH
# OF AN
# ANGEL

Also by Frances & Richard Lockridge
in Thorndike Large Print

The Norths Meet Murder
Murder Is Served
Murder Within A Murder
The Dishonest Murderer
Death Takes A Bow
Death Has A Small Voice

The Production Review Committee of N.A.V.H.
has found this book to meet its criteria
for large type publications.

# Death of an Angel

A Mr. and Mrs. North Mystery

## Frances and Richard Lockridge

Thorndike Press • Thorndike, Maine

**Library of Congress Cataloging in Publication Data:**


Lockridge, Frances Louise Davis.
  Death of an angel : a Mr. and Mrs. North mystery /
Frances and Richard Lockridge. -- Large print ed.
    p.  cm.
  ISBN 1-56054-058-3 (alk. paper : lg. print)
  1. Large type books.  I. Lockridge, Richard, 1898-
II. Title.
[PS3523.O243D435  1990]                   90-44505
813'.54--dc20                              CIP

Thorndike Press Large Print edition published in 1990 by
arrangement with Harper & Row Publishers.


Cover design by James B. Murray.



**The tree indicium is a trademark of Thorndike Press.**



This book is printed on acid-free, high opacity paper. ∞

# DEATH
# OF AN
# ANGEL

# I

Naomi Shaw wore white — a white dinner dress which clung to her. She stood with her back to French doors, and her hands, held behind her, touched the doors, as if about to push them open. Her lovely chin was up a little and there was the look on her heart-shaped face, in her dark eyes, of one surprised by a great delight. Behind her, beyond the doors, a garden lay in moonlight. And then Naomi Shaw spoke, in that voice so widely considered beyond description.

"I've got — " she said, and there was the check there — the indescribable check. "I've *got* to remember Pudgy."

The thousand-odd people who sat (or stood) in front of her became breathless with laughter. They turned red with laughter; they clutched the area of their diaphragms. They held on to their knees; they leaned back in their seats. They wiped their eyes. The curtain came down on the second act of *Around*

7

*the Corner,* and the thousand-odd laughed on, and clapped their hands together and made small, strange sounds of utter happiness. House lights came up, a little slowly, as if reluctant to intrude. People looked at one another and said, "Oh. *Oh!*" Pamela North, one in from the aisle, sixth row center, looked at Gerald North, on the aisle, and saw him blurriedly through the tears of laughter. "Oh," Pamela North said. "Oh! *Jerry!*"

"Got to remember Pudgy," Gerald North said, and shook again. *"Pudgy!"*

"I know," Pam said. "Of all things! And even when you know it's coming — " Words failed Pamela at this point. They returned to her. "Somehow," she said, "it's better each time, isn't it? Shall we go have a cigarette?"

They went, more slowly with each step, up an aisle which clogged with men and women, most of whom continued to laugh, to say, *"Pudgy!"* to one another and, on that magic word, to laugh again. They reached the head of the aisle, and a man who stood there, clutching the rail with both hands, looked at them and shook his head. He had a long, sad face. It did not appear that he had heard, or seen, anything to laugh at. He spoke to the Norths.

"They think it's funny," he said. "Why? That's all I want to know. What's so damned funny about it?"

8

He looked anxiously at Pam, as anxiously at Jerry.

"It's the way she says it," he told them. "It's got to be that, hasn't it? Hasn't it? Because what else is so damned funny?"

"Everything," Pam said. "Just everything, Sammy. The way — the way it keeps coming up. I mean *every*thing keeps coming up."

"The running gag," Samuel Wyatt said. He shook his sad head. "*You* tell me, Jerry."

But he did not look, now, at Gerald North. He looked at the flushed faces of those coming up the aisles. He seemed to look in wonderment.

"Come on," Jerry said. "Let's get out of this. Out on the sidewalk."

He put a hand on the shoulder of Samuel Wyatt, playwright, and Wyatt permitted himself to be led away. He seemed to move in a daze, to grope his way through the crowded lobby, into the warm June night of Forty-third Street. He took the cigarette Jerry North offered him and stared at it, as if its use were beyond conception.

"In your mouth," Pam explained, slowly and carefully. "One end. You light the other. See?"

She demonstrated.

"You knew it was funny when you wrote it," Gerald North told Wyatt.

9

"Did I write it?" Wyatt said. "Pinch me."

"All right," Pam said, and did. Wyatt said, "Ouch!" but his heart was not in it.

"A hundred times," he said. "A *hundred times* she's said, 'Pudgy,' and every time — every *damned* time — they fall apart. Do you realize it's been a hundred times? Tonight."

It was, Pam told him, a delightful play. And Naomi Shaw was —

"Delectable," Wyatt said. " 'Since Miss Shaw is delectable,' Brooks Atkinson said. And Dick Watts said she was a lovely girl."

"Broth of a girl, surely," Jerry said.

"Just lovely girl," Wyatt told him. "You could hear the 'r's' rolling, of course."

"Mr. Nathan said she was a dish," Pam told them. "He liked the play, too. Everybody liked the play. You know that, Sammy."

"Why?" Samuel Wyatt enquired. "That's all I want to know. Every night — every other night, anyway — I come here and stand back there and look at them, and I still don't get it."

"It's funny," Jerry said. "You wrote a very funny play, Sam."

"I suppose so," Wyatt said. "I don't remember. It must have been funny, mustn't it? I watch the damned thing and watch it, and I say, 'Sure, it's got to be funny. Sure it has,' and — The hell with it. I'll buy you drinks.

Champagne. Very, very, *very* old cognac."

"No," Jerry said. "We're going back. You're not?"

"Never," Wyatt said. "So help me, Jerry. Never. Until tomorrow night, anyway." Abruptly, he snapped his fingers. A buzzer sounded. He snapped his fingers again, but did not seem conscious that he did so. The crowd on the sidewalk began to thin. Wyatt took several quick, almost jerky, steps, away from the Norths. He stopped and came back.

"You coming to this binge?" he demanded.

"I don't — " Jerry began, and Pam said, "Of course, Sammy. Aren't you? But of course you are."

Wyatt gestured, again abruptly, both hands raised to the level of his head, fingers spread. He started away again, and now the Norths turned toward the theater doors. They looked back. Wyatt smiled at them suddenly, the smile very wide on his long and narrow face. He waved. He went.

"Writers are strange things, aren't they?" Pam said.

"Yes," Jerry said.

They went down the aisle, found their seats. The house lights were still up.

"Has he always been like this?" Pam asked.

A good deal like this, Jerry told her. When Wyatt was a novelist — merely a novelist — it

11

had been very hard to get him to read proofs. When he was got to read them, it was very hard to prevent him from rewriting, in entirety; a practice of which publishers disapprove.

"Once he's done with anything, he hates it," Jerry said. "Sees no possible good in it. If critics like it, the critics are fools. If it sells, the public is a fool. Now he's got — this."

The lights began to dim.

"It must," Pam said, "be very baffling. It — "

The curtain began to rise. Somebody behind Pamela North said, "Shh-h!"

Naomi Shaw was lying, face down, on beach sand. She extended brownly and beautifully from a white bathing suit. (It had been at this moment of the play, some weeks previously, that a gentleman on convention had risen from his second row seat, held arms out in entreaty and bellowed. It had been necessary to remove him, but sympathy had been widespread.) It occurred to Pam, now, that her husband's lips moved, although he made no sound. It was to be presumed that he merely moistened them. A very tall, very tanned, very handsome young man, wearing bathing trunks, entered, stage left. Naomi rolled onto her back, like a kitten, and looked up at the man. (From the rear of the balcony, someone whis-

12

tled softly.) Naomi spoke. . . .

At last the curtain stayed down. Naomi had bowed, holding the hand of a blond girl, slightly taller than she, in another fashion — but how ordinary were all other fashions! — lovely. She had bowed with handsome man and blond girl held in either hand; she had bowed with the entire company, which, stretched in line across the stage, was more numerous than anyone had remembered. She had bowed alone. She had bowed again. But then the curtain was adamant.

"Do you," Jerry said, as they stood on the sidewalk, "do you really want to go to this brawl?"

"Yes," Pam said. "I'd love to."

They had time to kill. They went to the lobby of the Algonquin, where time dies easily, without protest. They sipped scotch and plain water.

"The money," Pam said, "must simply be pouring in, mustn't it?"

"To Wyatt?"

"To everybody," Pam said. "To Mr. Strothers and — oh, everybody. Even, in a small way, us." But she paused, then. "Only," she said, "it doesn't, does it? Oughtn't there to be just a trickle? After all, five hundred dollars is five hundred dollars. I'm still surprised at us."

Jerry was also surprised at them. Never before had the Norths spread the wings of theatrical angels — or, a little more accurately, cherubim. But Samuel Wyatt was a friend, as well as author — and author who actually sold — on the list of North Books, Inc. He was also persuasive. And the Norths had liked the play, even in type — even without (although now that was unthinkable) Naomi Shaw. It still surprised them, nevertheless, that they had invested five hundred dollars in *Around the Corner*.

"When the profits start," Jerry explained. "Strothers has to pay off the cost of production. The nut, they call it. Then profits. Then our trickle."

He meant, Pamela supposed — with some incredulity — that the nut wasn't paid off yet? After all those weeks, after the hundredth performance, when you still had to wait weeks and weeks for tickets?

It wasn't, Jerry pointed out, a cheap production. It was not a cheap show to keep running. Money poured in; money also poured out. But it was about time for profits. Jasper had said that only yesterday.

"Jasper?" Pam said.

She was told she remembered; she was told that nobody could forget. Jasper. Jasper Tootle.

"It's just," Pam said, "that I don't like to believe it. Why Tootle?"

Jasper Tootle came, Jerry explained gently, from a long line of Tootles. It was a name like any other name. As a literary agent for, among many others, Samuel Wyatt, Jasper had made it widely known.

"Has he got money in it, too?"

Jerry thought he had. He said a good many people had.

"And Mr. Strothers himself?"

Wesley Strothers, producer of *Around the Corner* had put into it everything he could scrape together. At least, he had told Wyatt so; told Wyatt so frequently; told him sometimes with passion. (The passion had arisen when Wyatt had proved reluctant to make changes which Strothers knew — but *knew* — would make all the difference. "The general idea was," Wyatt had told Jerry, who now told Pam, "that Wyatt was trying to send him to the poorhouse.")

"Well," Pam said, "it's turning out nice for everybody. Hadn't we better go?"

They went.

When a play achieves its hundredth performance, the theatrical columnists report a "milestone," being dedicated to the verbally familiar. Somebody provides a party for the cast, the producer, such angels as may be in the vicinity, and friends of friends. To such celebrations, even the author of the play frequently is invited. It is true that these traditional festivals vary somewhat in brightness since, with plays as with people, it is not only where you've got, but your condition on arrival. Now and then a play is glassy-eyed at the milestone, and staggers to it, hands extended gropingly toward Hollywood. But others approach grandly, and of this group *Around the Corner*, that pleasant June evening, was one.

It had run its hundred, and might well run forever. It had, to be sure, a cast of eleven, and was a three-setter, of which the beach set of the last act was the most troublesome. (Sand gets into everything.) Phyllis Barnscott, the second lead, did not come cheap and Sidney Castle likewise knew his value by the week. Naomi Shaw's check (even before her percentage of the gross) was signed by Wesley Strothers with averted eyes. His signature quivered, had nothing of the boldness evident, for example, on the check made out to Jane Lamont, who might, except that she understudied Naomi and so had to stick around, have gone home midway of the second act.

But the gross was the thing, and for weeks it had hardly wavered. One thousand and sixty-two people could sit in the Forty-third Street Theater, and some would stand. In a

16

week they could pay $33,500 for the privilege. Even in Holy Week, the gross had dipped only into the upper twenties and in the week after Easter there were standees in layers, and even the boxes were filled by those who felt that half of *Around the Corner* was better than none. Tickets for October were at the printers; tickets for August were selling nicely. The sky, in short, was cloudless. And Bradley Fitch was giving the party, in his duplex on Park Avenue.

In the taxicab, Pam North pointed out, with doubt in her voice, that they were not dressed. She dangled this, however, only briefly, pulling in just before Jerry — who is not essentially a party man — snapped. It didn't really, Pam said, matter. Jerry raised his eyebrows.

"We're the literary element," Pam said. "Like Sammy. Nobody will expect anything." To this, Jerry said, "Oh," and the cab stopped. A doorman, white-gloved against the contamination of taxis and other creeping things, opened the door for them. He waited, detached, tolerant, while Jerry paid. But he walked across the sidewalk with them, and held open a heavy glass door. He could hardly have done more had they arrived properly, chauffeur-driven.

They joined a tall, dark man who stood, a little stooped, waiting the arrival of an elevator. He looked at them from dark eyes, over

17

which the brows jutted. He looked at them, for a second, as if somewhat puzzled. But then he said, "Oh, hello. Glad you could make it." Then he looked around the lobby. "Didn't bring Sam with you?"

"Bring Sam?" Pamela said. "Why bring Sam, Mr. Strothers? That is — "

The elevator door opened.

"Foolish thing to say," Wesley Strothers said, and stood back to let them go ahead into the car. "Somehow got the idea you were — oh. Remember now. Saw you talking to him in front of the theater. Got the idea you were together."

"We ran into him," Jerry said.

"Writers I don't get," Strothers said. "Morbid, that's what they are. Ever notice that, South?"

"North," Jerry said. "Yes, or ebullient. Or, for the most part, just like anybody else."

"Not our Sammy," Strothers said. "This is where we get out. You know Fitch?"

"No," Jerry said. "Somebody called and invited us. I suppose Sam suggested it."

Wesley Strothers, to this, made a sound without words. Pam led them into an ante-room, which appeared to be a living room, furnished with a sofa and two modern arm chairs. A wide door, painted a dusky red, was in the wall they faced. The elevator door closed behind them. It was of the width of the door opposite and painted the same color.

"Swank," Strothers said. His voice was low pitched, rumbled slightly. Yet laughter seemed to stir in it. "Do you well here, as Brad says. Also calls it his little *pied-à-terre*. Quite a boy, Brad is." He pressed a button beside the red door, and musical notes occurred within. "Nice boy, all the same," Strothers said, and the door opened. " 'Evening, Henry," Strothers said, to a butler in a black coat. "Party started?"

"Oh, yes, Mr. Strothers," Henry said. "It has indeed, sir."

It had indeed. It had started in a big room beyond the entrance foyer — a room, Pam thought suddenly, too large for anything she could think of. It had — for heaven's sake, Pam thought. *There's a chandelier!* There was. It was prismed.

"Used to be his mother's apartment," Strothers said. "Accounts for everything."

A tall man — tall and broad of shoulder and tapering down — left a group which was under the chandelier, and came forward. He advanced a hand. He told Pam that she must be Mrs. North. He said he had heard so much about her. She admitted that she was; did not ask what he had heard, or from whom. He said, "Bradley Fitch. Glad you could come.

19

Mr. North, sir. 'Lo, Wes," thus taking care of everyone. Momentarily, then, he looked over them, toward the door from the foyer. He smiled and nodded over them, but briefly. He waved to a large man, probably in his middle fifties, whose round, pink face had been touched soothingly by many barbers, who had the most dignified of double chins. The woman with him, who was blond and much younger, who was the second lead in *Around the Corner* — why can't I ever remember names when I ought to? Pam demanded of herself — came just to his shoulder.

"Ah," the tall man said. "Gerald, my boy. Been hoping you'd turn up." His smile, which was all affability, encompassed the others. "And this is the little lady." He extended a hand, which Pam accepted. It was a plump hand, but firm. It appeared that she was the little lady in question.

"Tootle," the big man said. "Jasper Tootle," and to this Pam said, "Oh. Of course." It did, for some reason, seem inevitable.

"Where's Naomi?" Strothers said, and spoke to the blond girl, who was much, Pam thought, more exciting to look at now that the Naomi enquired of was not beside her.

"Taking a shower, darling," the blonde said, and then, "I'm Phyllis Barnscott," to Pamela and Gerald North. Fitch said, "Oh, sorry. I'm a hell of a host," and the Norths identified themselves. Fitch looked around the big room and made gesturing motions, emphatically, with his head, and a waiter brought a tray. On the tray, champagne bubbled coolly in wide glasses. Phyllis said, "Ummm!" and reached. Phyllis had, Pam North realized suddenly, an amusing face.

"Nobody has to drink this stuff," Fitch told them. "There's plenty of everything."

There was indeed, Pam thought, and sipped champagne.

"Excuse me a minute, cousins," Bradley Fitch said, and went elsewhere, and Phyllis Barnscott moved beside Pam North.

"You're friends of Sammy's, aren't you?" she said. She looked around the room. "He'll never come, will he? There's just too much of everything for Sammy."

"He — " Pam said, and broke off and said, "He just *has* come." Phyllis turned, too, and they watched Samuel Wyatt, who stood inside the door from the foyer. He was a slight man, he wore a dark suit which fitted him limply, on his long face there was an expression of incredulity. He stood alone, and snapped the fingers of his right hand.

"If somebody doesn't do something," Phyllis Barnscott said, "he'll just go away again, won't he?" She raised her voice a little, pro-

21

jecting it a little. "Sammy," she said. "It's all right, son."

Samuel Wyatt appeared, at first, to blink. But then he smiled, and walked to them through deep carpet. "A friendly face," Sam said. "Two friendly faces." He said, "I — "

A slender woman in her forties came from somewhere and said:

"Mr. Wyatt. It must be Mr. Wyatt, isn't it?"

"Yes," Wyatt said.

"I'm Alicia Nelson," she said, and to this Wyatt said, "Oh." Then he said, "Oh, of course."

"You've never heard of me," she said. "Why should you have?" She looked at Wyatt's long face, which did not display any inclination to contradict. "I'm Brad's cousin," Alicia Nelson said. She smiled briefly. "Really his cousin. When I heard he was giving this" — she indicated this — "I said I simply had to come. I said I had to meet the man who wrote that perfectly *wonderful* play."

"Oh," Wyatt said. "Well, I — "

"Do you speak?" she said, then. She had an expression of great eagerness. Her short gray hair curled vigorously.

There was no doubt, this time, that Samuel Wyatt blinked.

"She means at things, don't you, Mrs. Nelson?" Phyllis Barnscott said. "He's easily baffled, Mrs. Nelson. Luncheons, Sammy. Women's clubs. I'm Phyllis Barnscott. I'm in Mr. Wyatt's play."

It was Alicia Nelson, this time, who said, "Oh"; who paused a moment and said, "I *know*, my dear." She looked at Pamela North, who said, "I'm Pamela North. I don't do anything, really."

"No, I'm afraid I don't," Samuel Wyatt said, and snapped fingers of his right hand. "Why?"

"The club," Mrs. Nelson said. "It's a country club but some of us feel — I mean, golf is wonderful, of course — and polo too. I don't really mean. But sometimes one wants more. Don't you think, Mr. Wyatt?"

"I'm afraid," Samuel Wyatt said, "that I've never played polo, Mrs. Nelson. I'm afraid of horses."

"Of horses?" she said. Then she laughed. "Oh," she said. "I should have known." She did not say what she should have known. "I —"

But Jasper Tootle loomed, and now a small young woman, very pretty, very red of hair — and, Pam thought, smelling very wonderful — was with him. It was one of the other women in the play — oh, yes, the one who dropped her drink and then — Jane Lamont,

23

that was who it was.

"Sam, my boy," Jasper said, and spoke heartily. "Wondered where you'd got to."

"Here," Sam Wyatt said, and looked around him. "Just here, Jasper. This is Mrs. Nelson. Jasper Tootle."

Jasper Tootle was charmed. He said as much.

"I'm Mr. Wyatt's agent, Mrs. Nelson," he said. "Have to keep an eye on him. It's a delightful party, isn't it? Your cousin's quite a boy."

It was to be expected that Jasper Tootle would have informed himself. Why, Pam thought, don't I, ever?

"Tootle," Mrs. Nelson said. "The Rye Tootles?"

"Omaha," Jasper said. "I know Henry, of course. No relation, I'm afraid."

There was, briefly, a pause.

"Mrs. Nelson wants Sammy to talk," Phyllis said. "To a group."

Jasper Tootle was seldom speechless. This seemed to leave him so. He looked at Wyatt, who, expression absent from his long face, was looking around the room. The room, large as it was, was now almost filled.

"I don't think Sammy likes to make speeches," he said. "Do you, my boy?"

"What?" Wyatt said. He focused on Alicia

Nelson. "I'm afraid of speeches, too," he said. "Where's Nay, Jasper? Isn't she coming?"

"Sure she is," Jasper Tootle said. "She'll — "

But Pam North saw Jerry, who was holding a glass in either hand, who was looking around.

"An entrance, Sammy," Phyllis said. "We actresses — "

Pam made an exit. She joined Jerry; hoped the glass was for her, was assured it was. She was asked if she was having a good time.

"Not terribly," Pam said. "It's all like the opening chorus, isn't it? Except they don't sing."

Jerry shook his head at that. He edged them into a corner.

"Before the star comes on," Pam said. "When they're all saying, 'He comes, he comes.' Or she, of course. And you get tired of waiting."

They could go, Jerry said. Nobody would mind.

"It wouldn't be right," Pam said. "Not before Miss Shaw comes. She hasn't, you know."

Jerry did not know. All he knew, at the moment, was that one of Jasper's boys had a book manuscript that Jerry was going to be crazy about. Although Harpers had not been, nor Doubleday. Nor, in fact, Simon and Schuster.

"I do hope," Pam said, "that nothing has

25

happened to her."

She was invited not to be morbid.

"It's the champagne," Pam said. "I never know why, because it's supposed to be so gay. And all it makes me is sad." She paused. "Not even tight," she added.

She had had one glass, Jerry pointed out. A glass and a sip, and otherwise since dinner only an enfeebled scotch. She expected too much. "Gaiety," Pam said. "The fabulous life. The glitter of the world of the theater." She looked around. "It's just people, isn't it?" she said.

"Now," Jerry said, "you're really being morbid."

It was only, Pam said, that realism kept cropping up. She sipped. They were protected in their corner; they could watch the play. The cast of the play was large — there were fifty people in the oversize room, with the prismed chandelier sparkling discreetly in its center. There were men in business suits, and some in jackets and slacks; there were a few in dinner jackets, of which Bradley Fitch's and those of one or two others were white. The women shone more; by and large the women glowed, and not a few of them were close enough to beauty — Phyllis Barnscott, the vividly red-haired Jane Lamont. "There's Leonard Lyons," Pam said, and there, indeed, was Mr. Lyons.

And there was the handsome couple which put forward Hollywood's best matrimonial feet, having been in step — now — for almost a year. There was — surely that was the man who wrote — And wasn't she — but of course she was.

And all the fifty — the more than fifty — talked. It was inconceivable, from the sound, that they did not all talk at once. The voices of the women were jagged above the heavier monotone of the men — it was as if serrated hills rose from a plain. Momentarily, there was the famous laugh — the laugh known to everyone who had entered a theater, watched a comedy program on television. Speaking of television, wasn't that one of the ones Godfrey had fired?

"I," Pam North said, "feel like a tourist. Do you?"

Jerry did, a little.

"I wish," Pam said, "the parade would come. Don't you?"

Because there was, about the now lively enough — and noisy enough — party, a curiously tentative air. It was as if, for all vivacity brought to bear (and in most cases vivacity most professionally designed) nobody's heart was in it. No conversation (but this was only to be felt; could not be demonstrated) progressed with security, was in a real sense engaged in. People talked with the major portions of their minds elsewhere, waiting for something different. Pam said something to this effect.

"People do, at parties," Jerry said. "Especially people on display. You know that."

She did. But it was more than that. She was certain it was more than that.

"Probably," Jerry said. "It's in your own mind." He gestured; a waiter presented a tray; they exchanged empty glasses for glasses that bubbled. Bradley Fitch was passing; he stopped. "Making out all right, cousins?" he asked, and beamed at them. "Wonderfully," Pam said. "It's a wonderful party." Fitch went on. He was a large man; he moved with remarkable grace. "Like a big cat," Pam said. "They'll all be very annoyed at us."

"They," Jerry said, "will be asleep on all the chairs they are supposed to stay off of. Leaving cat hair."

That the Norths' three cats would be doing precisely that was obvious; that they would, in time, arise to express the vociferous protest of abandoned Siamese equally went without saying.

"Now," Pam said, "we're doing it. Where *is* Miss Shaw? Because that's it, isn't it? It's her party, more than Mr. Strothers'. More even than Sammy's. What is there about her?"

"She's good-looking," Jerry said. "She's a good actress. I don't mean a Helen Hayes, but — "

Pam was shaking her head. He stopped.

"There's more than that," Pam said.

"Sure," Jerry said. "The indescribable something, and I quote from somebody."

"From everybody," Pam said. "She — " Pam stopped. She was looking toward the door from the foyer. There was a stir there. Bradley Fitch, tall enough to show above the others, seemed the center of the stir.

But he was not. The stir moved into the room, and now most of those in the room were aware of it. And Fitch was not the center — or was, at best, a segment of the center, an adjunct of the center.

The center was a small and beautifully arranged young woman in a gold evening dress which left perfect shoulders bare. The center was a young woman of twenty-five, born Mary Shaftlich on Independence Avenue in Kansas City, Missouri, daughter of the manager of a chain grocery store; graduate of Northeast High School, where she had "taken elocution" and of the Heart of America Business College, from which she had emerged as an only moderately competent stenographer. The center was, in other words, Naomi Shaw.

"Why," Pam North said, looking at Naomi

across the room, "she's really gay, isn't she?"

Sometimes one may toss a single match into a smoldering fire, and find that flame leaps up. Sometimes a party comes alight. . . .

"It's a wonderful party," Pam North was saying, half an hour later, this time to a handsome young man named Sidney Castle — who danced perfectly — and this time meaning it. There had been another room behind the big room with the chandelier, and here the floor was bare and polished, and here there was a small orchestra. (And another bar. Mr. Fitch did things perfectly; that could no longer be denied.) Voices were generally somewhat louder by then, but they seemed (which was absurd) to have become more melodious.

"Tops," Sidney Castle said. "Absolutely tops."

It was, Pam thought absently, not so much what he said as the way he said it. He was a very expert dancer; she could look anywhere she liked. She could see Jerry dancing with — oh yes, that Mrs. Nelson. And there was dear old Jasper with — why, that was the girl with the famous laugh. She looked much smaller in real life, and much prettier, too. And Sam Wyatt — Sam of all people! — was dancing with Naomi Shaw, who was laughing at something he had said and looked, in that instant, as she must have looked at the Junior Prom at

Northeast High (only rather differently dressed, of course) and seemed without pretense. And there was —

The music stopped. Sidney Castle bowed. He was an expert bower, too. Jerry came toward them and he had the expression — but how *could* he have? — of a man who is beginning to think it's about time to go home. And then —

A horn in the little orchestra sounded "Attention!" — sounded it softly, almost tenderly. And now Naomi Shaw was standing beside, not Sam Wyatt, but Bradley Fitch, and they were — they certainly were — a most beautiful couple.

" — says it's all right," Bradley Fitch said, and his face was a little flushed, and it appeared he had begun speaking before he planned. He stopped, and put an arm around Naomi's perfect shoulders, and drew her closer.

"Want everybody to know," Bradley Fitch said. "Nay and I — we're going to get married next week." He looked around. "Going to steal your girl, cousins," he said.

There was a kind of tingle in the air.

"Put her in my pocket," Fitch said, and the delight was evident in his voice. He did, then, lift her off her feet. She laughed, her perfect arms around his neck.

It was very young, Pam thought. It was

very charming. It was —

A stocky man in his middle thirties turned suddenly and walked out of the room. He did not dramatize the action. He merely went. A few noticed him, Pam North among them. But, by then, most were drinking to the health and happiness of Naomi Shaw and Bradley Fitch, who had more money than it was easy to think of, a seven-goal handicap in polo and now — and now the "delectable" star of *Around the Corner*.

# II

*Friday, 5:45 P.M. to 8:10 P.M.*

Jerry North, being trained, had given warning, although it was brief. He was bringing Sam Wyatt home with him for a drink. He had said, "Be with you in a minute, Sam," from which Pam deduced that Wyatt was, politely, absenting himself from Jerry's private office while Jerry spoke, privately, with his wife. "Needs his hand held," Jerry said. "Although why he came to me. All right?"

It was of course all right, although Pam made no promise of dinner to follow drinks. "Lamb chops," Pam said, putting the matter in a nutshell. Lamb chops, as is known to all, cannot be stretched. Jerry said that they would see, which in domestic shorthand meant that they could go out to dinner, if it came to that, which meant that Martha, who cooked for the Norths, would be left somewhat in mid-air. To the smallest things, Pam told the cats, there are ramifications, and went to the kitchen to inform Martha of this new uncertainty. She returned, and decided to change her dress. The

33

cats accompanied her and sat, two on a bed and one on the dressing table, staring with round blue eyes, as if never before had they seen any action so incomprehensible.

Just before Pam heard Jerry's key in the lock, the three cats turned their heads simultaneously toward the hallway which led to the living room, which was where the door was. This meant that they had heard footsteps in the outside hall. But they did not leap from perches and gambol down the hallway, which meant that they had heard alien footsteps, along with those of Jerry, and chose to bide their time. The cat called Gin had been ill, and visited by a veterinarian, so that now any unaccounted-for arrival might presage a hypodermic needle in the rump. To all things, there are ramifications.

Pam went down the hallway, and went quickly, although she did not gambol. Sam Wyatt's face seemed to have increased in length. To her greeting he slightly shook his head and said, " 'Lo, Pam," in a tone of gloom. "Man needs a drink," Jerry said, from behind Sam Wyatt. "And how," Sam Wyatt said, with a falling inflection. He snapped the thumb and middle finger of his right hand, soundlessly. "Can't think why I keep doing that," he said, and looked at the hand with reproach. "Compulsion, probably. Means something, I shouldn't wonder." He paused. "Something dire, no doubt," he added. He looked at Pam and shook his head again.

"It's all gone down the drain," he said.

"I'm terribly sorry," Pam said. "What?"

"Everything," Sam said. "Can I have a scotch on the rocks?"

He could. He did. They sat, the Norths with martinis.

"Six per cent of thirty thousand dollars," Sam Wyatt said. "Thirty-two, one week. Less the ten, of course. A *week*. And then — "

And then, quite unexpectedly, he sniffled. He sniffled again. His eyes filled with tears and Pam, keeping a bright, and she hoped sympathetic, smile, thought, well, *really*.

The wife of a publisher meets writers from time to time, and this is inescapable. Writers often need their hands held and publishers occasionally oblige. Publishers must attend literary cocktail parties, and take their wives, and at such festivals writers are every now and then encountered. So for the breed, Pamela North, of all human idiosyncrasy tolerant, had acquired a special tolerance. But this — this carried it far. Even if things went down drains, did grown men weep into their scotch? It appeared, lamentably, that they did.

Sam Wyatt drew out a handkerchief, and dabbed his eyes. He sniffled further, and dabbed his nose. And then he stood up, and looked around. And then, a little wildly, he pointed toward the door which opened on the hallway to the bedroom, and said, in a choked voice, "Damn. Oh, damn." And then he sneezed.

Martini, the older of the cats, the mother of the others, had come to scout. It might not be the vet; it had not sounded like the vet. It might be — At the sneeze, which was convulsive, Martini flattened pointed, dark brown ears. She spoke once, with emphasis. She turned, and stalked away, no doubt to warn her offspring. And Sam Wyatt turned to Jerry and said, still in a choking voice, "You've *got them!*"

The Norths merely looked at him.

"*Cats!*" Sam Wyatt said. His eyes were streaming, now. "Of all things — *cats!* Don't you know they're worse than horses?"

"Than — " Pam said. "Than *horses*, Mr. Wyatt? I mean — horses in an apartment? I mean — "

She stopped, being unable, at the moment, to mean anything at all.

But Jerry said, "Damn. You've told me. I'd forgotten." He turned to Pam. "Got to get him out of here," he said. "Dandruff, you know."

"Dan — " Pam began, and said, "*Oh!* How dreadful! And we're simply swarming with

36

them. I'm so —"

"Wah-ugh," Sam Wyatt said.

" — should have remembered," Pam said, to Sam Wyatt with sympathy, to Gerald North with reproach. She raised her voice. "We have to go, Martha," she called. "The chops tomorrow or something. Will you feed the —" She stopped. Perhaps even the word. "Martini and you know," she said. "We —"

But by then Jerry had led Sam Wyatt to the door, and Pam followed. Wyatt sneezed briskly, now, and it was doubtful whether he could see. It was almost half an hour, in the dry coolness of a cocktail lounge, before Sam Wyatt could finally blink away the tears. By then he had, in what voice he could manage, apologized, had assured them that he liked cats, that it was he who should have remembered.

"Is it only cats?" Pam asked, then, and Wyatt shook his head sadly.

It was a lot of things. Cats were the worst, he told them. But horses were bad, also. And even dogs, although less immediately, with somewhat less violence, had the same result.

"Mental, I suppose," Sam Wyatt said, in a tone of enhanced gloom. "Goes back to my childhood, probably. Cat-block. Probably a cat scratched me when I was — oh, two, maybe — and I got it confused with my mother. Things happen that way, they say."

This Pam doubted, intensely.

"You'd have had to be scratched by a horse, too, wouldn't you?" she said. "I don't think horses — anyway, that would be ailurophobia. The cat part, at least. And you're not afraid of them."

"I am of horses," Wyatt said. "I'm an equinophobe."

"It's a sensitivity," Pam said. "Lots of people have it. Jerry and I know a man who's that way about face powder. It makes things terribly difficult, of course."

"God," Wyatt said, and snapped his fingers. "Married man?"

"How could he be?" Pam said.

Wyatt said he saw what she meant. He sighed deeply, and it was evident that, in air again breathable, he had reverted to a more basic sorrow. He finished his scotch, lapping the Norths. He beckoned a waiter, and pointed at the empty glass.

"May as well while I can afford it," he said. He looked at the top of the table. "Wes'll have to close the play," he said. "Nothing else to do. All on account of Rover boy, with his mouth full of silver spoons. His I'm-going-to-put-this-little-girl-in-my-pocket." He snapped his fingers. "*My* play," he said. "This *polo* player Wes was so thick with."

He drummed on the table.

"What's so special about marriage?" he demanded.

There was a slight pause before Jerry said that a good many people found it rather interesting. Wyatt dismissed such people with another snap — another almost soundless snap — of his right thumb and middle finger. Then he went on, talking to the table top.

In spite of the notice, duly served, that Naomi Shaw was to be pocketed by Bradley Fitch, none of them had at first been too much concerned. Naomi wanted to marry her handsome, and noticeably wealthy, polo player. This was reasonably all right with everybody. It was obvious folly to marry outside the profession, but Nay would have to make her own mistakes. "You'd have thought she'd have learned, but there it is," Wyatt said, and went on without immediate explanation.

She would want a vacation. This they had all supposed — they being Strothers, Wyatt himself, and the others involved with *Around the Corner*, including the ten other members of the cast. They would close for — oh, for July and August; being generous. There was no danger that *Around the Corner* would be forgotten during a summer hibernation. They would reopen after Labor Day. It would be a nuisance, obviously. There would be the troublesome matter of refunds on tickets already sold. Not all the members of the cast wanted payless months, and there would be adjustments called for. But love must be permitted to conquer something, if not all.

This moderately sanguine view of matters had lasted only until about one-thirty that afternoon, midway in a luncheon at Sardi's — a luncheon ostensibly as further celebration of the betrothal ("Naomi Shaw and Brad Fitch to hitch" — Leonard Lyons in *The New York Post*), but also for discussion of the future of the play. Fitch and Naomi had, Wyatt reported, held hands under the table; he and Wesley Strothers had not. At a certain stage in the luncheon they had, instead, begun to wave their hands.

Fitch had thought, he said, that they had understood. Naomi was quitting the stage. Period. They were going to France in mid-July and after that — well, Fitch said, there was no telling.

"He was full of that goddamned charm," Wyatt said, and finished his new scotch and snapped his fingers. He did not, this time, snap them silently. "He made it sound so goddamned reasonable. And, kept calling us 'cousins.'"

From Bradley Fitch's point of view, Pam thought, listening, it no doubt was reasonable. From his point of view, the theater was all very well. It was something Nay had enjoyed — a little, probably, as years before she might have enjoyed playing with dolls. But now she would put all this away, for something "real."

"*Real!*" Wyatt said. "The — the *polo player!*"

It had not been necessary for Fitch to point out that Naomi would not, hereafter, need to earn a living. The salary (and percentage) which had so often caused Strothers' hand to shake would need to be no drop in the Fitch bucket. They would, Fitch had said, see how it was. He had looked at Naomi fondly. "Want to have my girl around," he said. "Need her to look after me."

"Yah!" Sam Wyatt said at this point in his narrative. "The overgrown prep-school boy!"

"Of course," Pam said, gently, "you can see, Sam. Looked at one way, it's rather sweet."

Wyatt repeated this characterization as an expletive. Pam said, quickly, that she was sorry.

Of course, they had argued. They had argued and waved their hands. They had pointed out the loss to everyone — the loss of jobs to actors, of money to investors, of profits to producers and royalties to authors. Strothers

41

had gone further — he had talked of thousands, living drab lives, who had found, and might still find, bright escape in *Around the Corner*. They could not, selfishly, rob the world of laughter; they could not draw blackout curtains over this window on illusion; they could not —

"Quite a speech Wes made," Wyatt said, for the moment critical and detached. "Didn't know he had it in him. Damned near had me in tears. He got all through and this polo player says, 'Of course we're sorry about that, Wes. But I don't see what we can do.'"

Wesley Strothers had suggested several things, postponement of marriage was chief among them. Postponement for a year — what was a year? Or, at the least, for six months. Or — a vacation first, then six months, then — ?

"Sorry," Fitch said. "We've got it planned."

And then Fitch had made his suggestion. Couldn't they just get themselves "another girl"?

"That's what Nay's marrying," Wyatt said, and now his voice was merely hopeless. "Nay's just a girl. Girl he happens to have fallen for. Wouldn't you think she'd see?"

It appeared that she did not, or did not fully. She had, to be sure, widened her eyes somewhat at this suggestion from her beloved, and looked across the table at Strothers with the

42

smallest of grimaces. But she had remained tender toward Fitch, in spite of the affront — and the palpable ignorance. He was, her smiling lips said, just a great big boy; a great big *lovable* boy. Wyatt put his head briefly in his hands.

They had tried to explain that, when an actress has become a character, as Naomi Shaw had become the Lisa of *Around the Corner*, all illusion hangs on a single, silken thread. At the beginning it had not been so, of course. "The play's all right," Wyatt said. "It's a nice little play. I know that, whatever I say." At the beginning, they might, with luck, have found themselves another girl; opened with another girl. The results might not have been, as they had been with Naomi Shaw, phenomenal. But they might have been very pleasant. Somebody else might have become Lisa; not the same Lisa, but one of other charms. Pudgy might not have been so well remembered, but other qualities might have been found. Naomi Shaw had not been the only pretty young actress, with something a little fey in her playing — at the start she had not been.

"It's different with big shows," Wyatt said to them, digressing into shop talk — talk still a little new to him, and, therefore, the more to be prized. "Strong action show. Or a musical.

Take *The King and I* and Gertrude Lawrence dies and that breaks everybody's heart. And the show isn't the same, God knows, but you can keep it running."

But it was not that way with *Around the Corner*. You took Naomi Shaw out of it now, and the pretty iridescent little thing went "pouff!" "Wouldn't even leave a damp spot," Wyatt said, and lifted his empty glass and looked gloomily at the circle of moisture it had left on the table.

Failing with Fitch, they had turned to Naomi herself. "She's in the profession," Wyatt said. "She could understand what we were talking about."

Also, it was her career they were talking about. She had come a long way from Independence Avenue, in Kansas City, Missouri, from elocution lessons at Northeast High. There was every possibility that she might go further; even much further. Strothers had told her that, told all of it to her several times, urged her to think about what she was throwing away.

"To hear him, you'd have thought she was going to be Helen Hayes," Wyatt said. "Bernhardt, maybe. Duse. I think she's pretty good, but if Strothers meant half of it, he thinks she could be pretty great. He talked and talked and she said, 'I'm sorry, Wes. I've thought about all that. Don't think I haven't.' And then she looked at this damned polo player and —" Wyatt spread his hands. He snapped his fingers on both hands, simultaneously.

"She's in love," Pam North said, and Wyatt looked at her without belief and, in the voice of the doomed, called on the Deity.

"She's out of her mind," he said, then.

"Of course," Jerry said, "I don't know Miss Shaw. But Fitch has got a lot of money."

Pam looked at him in disappointment. And Wyatt shook his head. He said he wished it were that simple. He said he didn't think it was.

"At bottom she's a nice kid," he said. "Oh, she's been around. Been married before to some guy — can't think of his name. That blew up. Knows how to act. Well enough, anyway. Knows how to call everybody 'darling.' All the same, she's just a kid from the middle west. Where she picked up this special whatever-it-is she's got —" He ended that with a shrug. "What I'm getting at, I'm pretty sure she's not just working a gold mine."

"All right," Jerry said. "But it's a nice mine." Pam, nevertheless, shook her head at him, still disapproving. She said that he always thought the worst of people, and that she wished he wouldn't.

"All is love," Jerry said; and then, to Wyatt, "You got nowhere, then?"

They had got nowhere. They had kept at it until well along in the afternoon, and Naomi and Fitch had been patient with them. "Just kept on listening and being sorry, Fitch did," Wyatt told them. Late in the afternoon, they had been, unexpectedly, reinforced. Jasper Tootle had come in for a drink and, with him, G. K. Snaith. He appeared to assume the last name would have significance for the Norths. He found it did not.

"*Her* agent," he explained. "Flesh peddler. Artists' representative. Little, dried-up geezer — and he and Tootle make a hell of a funny pair, incidentally. First either of them had heard about this."

Tootle and G. K. Snaith had paused by the table; had begun conventional congratulations before they were stopped, a little peremptorily, by Wesley Strothers — stopped with the news.

"You're nuts," Snaith had told his client, and Tootle had said, "Now, children. We'll have to get *this* straightened out." The two agents had pulled up chairs, and everything already said had been said again, and still again. It had been after four when Fitch had stood, and pulled Naomi up beside him, and said, with a pleasant — or, as Wyatt called it, "that damned half-witted" — smile that he was sure they all understood one another. They did, by then. Strothers had gone one way, presumably to see that the closing notice was posted, in accordance with his contractual obligations. Snaith and Tootle had gone another, communing over lost percentages.

"Jasper's been getting a couple of hundred a week out of me, or damned near it," Wyatt said. "God knows what Snaith's been getting from Nay, with television appearances and all."

Wyatt had wandered, lonely and forlorn, thinking of six per cent of the gross (less ten), had thought of Jerry North and had applied for hand holding.

"Anyway," he said, "it looks like I'll have to go back to work."

He had thought Jerry would like to know that, and now Jerry said that he did, indeed.

"So let's go some place and — " Wyatt began, and stopped, and said, in a lower tone, "Well, well," and with a movement of his head, indicated a couple who were walking between tables, led by a waiter captain, toward a banquette.

The cocktail lounge was large and pleasant, cheerful and, for a cocktail lounge, well lighted. It was an amenity of a hotel on lower Fifth Avenue; it was, certainly, the reverse of surreptitious. And yet it was also, Pam North thought, one of the last places in which she would have expected to see Naomi Shaw — and, just possibly, one of the last places in which Naomi Shaw would expect to be seen.

But Pam saw her — the three of them saw her. The man with her was squarely built, almost stocky, not tall. He was square of shoulder and, from the rear, somewhat square of head. He walked behind the slight and lovely girl methodically, with resolution. The waiter captain pulled a table out and Naomi slid behind it, quickly and with grace. The man followed her and sat firmly, and at once turned toward her and began to talk. She looked down at the table as she listened.

The man's face was square — all of the man was square. His face was deeply tanned — so deeply tanned that its darkness was apparent even across the room, even in the soft lights of the room.

Jerry North looked at Wyatt and raised his eyebrows, and Sam Wyatt shook his head. "Never saw him before," Wyatt said. "Wonder what she did with the polo player?" He brightened. "Say!" he said. "You don't suppose — " But he dimmed in mid-sentence. "Not a prayer," he said. "Probably a cousin from Kansas. Getting a fill-in on romance."

But he did not seem to be, Pam North thought. It was he who talked and the girl who listened. She listened with little change of expression, and the expression unchanged was serious.

"I've got a feeling —" Pam began and Jerry, speaking quickly, said, "Yes, dear."

Pam was undeterred.

" — that I've seen him before," she said. "Recently. Just the — oh!" They waited. "Last night," Pam said. "This morning, really. At Mr. Fitch's party. He was —" She paused. "I remember now," she said. "Mr. Fitch made his announcement and that man" — she indicated with a movement of her head — "that man turned around and walked out." She nodded, confirming her own memory. "Stalked," she said. "If I ever saw a man stalk."

They all looked at the stocky man and Naomi Shaw. The two remained intent.

"I could have stalked myself," Wyatt said, abandoning the two across the room. "Are you going to have dinner with me?"

It appeared they were. They rode uptown to the Plaza and Wyatt — rather unexpectedly, to Pam — was known there. Of course, with six per cent of such a pleasant weekly gross, one might become known anywhere. All the same — the Plaza and Sam Wyatt. However —

They were at coffee when Sam Wyatt said,

after snapping his fingers, "This damned thing follows us around," and indicated a couple just coming into the room, being led toward a side table. Bradley Fitch was starting dinner late with his cousin Alicia Nelson.

That, Pam said, explained everything. When people were about to get married, there were always family things, cousins and the like. Naomi Shaw with hers, and now Fitch with his. It was —

She stopped, since she was not being listened to. Jerry was looking at Sam Wyatt, and Wyatt was looking across the room at Fitch. He was staring at Fitch, and seemed to have forgotten the presence of the Norths; his long face was set, and his eyes were narrowed.

"I wish to God," Sam Wyatt said, and spoke in a low tone, without inflection, "I wish to God she'd put poison in his soup."

Of course, Pam North thought, he doesn't mean it. He just looks as if he does.

# III

Mrs. Hemmins said, "Here, Toby. Here, Toby," and opened another door. She called with no great optimism, and opened the door with little hope. Once the big black long-hair got beyond the sitting room door, there was no telling where he would get to. Upstairs, likely as not. How was he to know that this wasn't an ordinary summer? Cats expect things to go on as they have gone on in the past, and certain matters cannot be made clear to them. Mrs. Hemmins had explained the whole situation to Toby a number of times, not really expecting him to understand — although he certainly *looked* as if he were understanding — but getting it out of her own system, in a manner of speaking. About changes in routine she felt a good deal as Toby did, and was at the further disadvantage of knowing how she felt, which presumably Toby did not.

If he was in the big kitchen, where he was not supposed to be, he was saying nothing

51

about it. "Here, Toby," Mrs. Hemmins said. "Nice Toby. Come here, boy." Nothing came. Mrs. Hemmins sighed and continued to look under things.

You could not reasonably blame Toby. This was the first June he could remember (Mrs. Hemmins supposed) when the two of them had not had the run of the apartment, if they wanted it. Toby usually did; Mrs. Hemmins was somewhat past the age for running. She, except for going out and coming in, and the weekly light cleaning which is all a place needs when it is shut up, stayed for the most part in her own sitting room, or bedroom, and did such cooking as she needed to do in the kitchenette. Where Toby went, in his somewhat formalized search for (she presumed) mice, was Toby's concern, so long as he did not get out of the apartment entirely, and did show up for meals. The chairs wore dust covers, so he could sleep where he chose — leaving long, silky hair to mark the places of his choice. If the mister decided to spend a day or two in town, there was ample warning. Usually he didn't, from late in May until October. And then he was in and out only a little more frequently, before he went to Florida, or Europe, or wherever he thought was a good place to go. All the staff except Mrs. Hemmins went back to the country house.

Why he had kept the place at all since the old lady died was more than Mrs. Hemmins could figure out. (She looked behind the range, where there was just room for Toby, but where Toby was not.) Sixteen rooms on two floors was ridiculous — why, it was bigger than any house ought to be, and it was only an apartment. (There is an essential absurdity in an apartment's being bigger than a house.) Even when the old lady was alive, and before that when they were both alive, it had been too big for any real use, and they'd never used more than half of it — the family *and* the help. It was a white elephant now. No mistake about that.

But, until this happened, Mrs. Hemmins had had no reason to complain, and so had complained only moderately. She had a roof over her head, and a place to have friends into. She had wages; she had an air-conditioning unit in her bedroom and another in the sitting room. All she really had to do was *be* there. She was, in a sense, a light left burning, an almost symbolic occupancy. She was bothered by no one.

And now he'd met this girl. This actress. Pretty enough, if you liked them skinny, and it seemed to Mrs. Hemmins — from what she read in the newspapers, saw pictured in the magazines — that nowadays men did. Nothing to do with her, in any case. But it did keep him in town, since the girl was in this play. (Mrs. Hemmins had seen the play; she, for one, didn't see why everybody made such a fuss about it.) Even on Saturdays, and she didn't suppose he'd been in New York on a Saturday more than once or twice in his life, until this came up.

Apparently, Toby was not in the kitchen, or if in the kitchen had found a new hiding place. She wouldn't put it past him. Well, if he were in the kitchen he'd eventually be yelling to get out. The only thing that mattered was that he hadn't gone upstairs. Not that that mattered too much. It was certainly time Mr. Fitch waked up, if he was going to. Out till all hours, of course, but here it was almost eleven.

Mrs. Hemmins went to the foot of the service stairs which led to the second floor of Bradley Fitch's duplex on Park Avenue, and called up them. "Toby," she called. "Come down here, Toby." Nothing came down there.

But then she heard, distantly, the upstairs doorbell and, waiting, heard footsteps. There was enough interval between the two to lead Mrs. Hemmins to the assumption that the doorbell had waked him up. And that meant that, before long, he would ring to have her bring breakfast up. (Not that there wasn't a perfectly good serving pantry up there, and all anybody would need to make breakfast for himself. But, when you had as much money as he had, she supposed you'd never think of that. Unless somebody stayed the night with you and got the breakfast for you.)

But, as she grumbled her way to the servants' sitting room, where the bell indicator was, Mrs. Hemmins was without animus toward Bradley Fitch. Employer or not, rich young man or not, nuisance or not, you couldn't help liking Mr. Bradley. Nobody could, so far as she'd ever noticed. . . .

The bell had awakened Bradley Fitch, in his large, and air-conditioned, bedroom on the second floor. Fitch groaned. Then he opened his eyes. Sitting on him, looking at him fixedly, was that Toby. Awake, Fitch discovered Toby was a heavy cat. He had supposed he was mostly fur. Fitch closed his eyes and groaned again, and opened them, and there was Toby.

Fitch was a horse and dog man. He had no fixed objection to cats, who were all right in their place. Their place was not on the abdomen of a human with a hangover. "Scat," Fitch said, and the effort amplified his headache. The word did not greatly interest Toby, since he considered it merely a word of greeting. ("Cat" was, of course, one of the several words Toby knew well. The slight hiss which this time preceded it could be ignored, and was.) The doorbell rang again.

"Oh, God," Fitch said, and started to get up. This Toby could not ignore. He protested, in a word, and got up himself. He was both quicker and more graceful than the man at getting up. "Who the hell?" Fitch said, dully, and found a robe, and went from his air-conditioned bedroom into an air-conditioned room, pleasantly furnished, which was called a "study" for want of a more appropriate word. The doorbell rang once more as, having crossed the study, Fitch went into the small foyer. Fitch opened the door. He blinked. He said, "Hello, cousin."

"Hope I'm not too early," his visitor said. "You said around eleven. It's a little after that."

"I said?" Fitch repeated. "Said what?"

"To come around," his visitor said. "Talk it over."

"I did?"

He was asked not to say he had forgotten. He was told that it had, after all, been his idea. "You said you'd been thinking it over, and there might be a way to work things out. Don't you remember?"

"No," Fitch said. "I'm sorry, cousin." He pressed his hands against his temples. "Seems to be a lot I don't remember," he said. "But — come on in."

The visitor came in.

"Fact is," Fitch said, "I seem to have tied one on. I've got the granddaddy of all hangovers."

The visitor was sympathetic.

"Tell you what, Brad," the visitor said. "I know a thing will fix you up."

"Coffee," Fitch said. "I'll have Rosie fix us up —"

"Better than coffee," his visitor said. "Tomato juice and — oh, several things. Tabasco. First you think you're on fire and then — like that — you're all right."

"God," Fitch said. "Sounds repellent, doesn't it?"

He was told to sit right there; just to sit right there and relax. He was told that his visitor knew where everything was — ought to, by now.

"All right," Fitch said, and sat in a deep chair. He leaned forward in it, his head in his hands. (At least, he supposed it was still his head.)

He tried to remember, and did not. Apparently, he had invited this. Got carried away, probably; got to feeling friends with the world. Said something he hadn't meant to say, the way people do. Tried to make every-

57

body happy, the way he sometimes did when he'd had a few more than usual. Well, he hadn't committed himself to anything, and nobody was going to make him believe he had. He —

"Here, Brad," his visitor said. "Drink this. Don't taste it. Just drink it." A tray with a glass on it was held within Fitch's uncertain vision. "Be a new man when you get that down," his visitor promised.

Fitch reached out a hand which trembled slightly and took the glass. He raised it, hesitantly, toward his lips.

"Drink up," his visitor told him. "That's the only way."

Fitch took a deep breath and let it out. He put the glass to his lips, and put his head back, and swallowed until there was nothing more to swallow. He almost choked over the last swallow.

"Think you're on fire is — " Fitch began. He did not finish. Surely, nothing could burn like this! If it was all Tabasco — if it was — *it can't burn like this. It can't be meant to —*

"Afraid I — " he managed to say, in a voice he had never heard before. He tried to get up. But he leaned forward in the chair. He vomited on the floor. . . .

The black cat looked at Fitch. The cat's whiskers flattened along his jaw, and the sensitive nostrils quivered. The cat laid back his rounded ears, and the cat's lips drew back so that sharp white teeth glinted into sight. But there was no one to see the cat. . . .

It was funny the mister didn't ring. Half an hour, now, since she'd heard him walking up there, after the doorbell rang. Usually he couldn't get his coffee fast enough. Probably whoever it was — and pretty early whoever it was — was holding things up. Maybe — maybe he'd gone out to breakfast with whoever it was. If that was what it was he might have told her. It wasn't like him to —

She heard the downstairs doorbell. Now what?

She had been in the kitchen. She had to walk through two large rooms to reach the entrance foyer. At the stairs she paused momentarily, since Toby was coming down them. Toby's tail was large. "You," she said. "You've been up to something, haven't you?"

It was apparent that Toby had. He completed his descent hurriedly, making himself small. On the floor, he ran, a cat hugging the surface — obviously, Mrs. Hemmins thought, a guilty cat. Or perhaps a frightened one. You might have thought that Mr. Bradley, finding him unwanted, had been harsh with him. Except that Mr. Bradley was not ever harsh with anyone. Better for him, probably, if he sometimes were. Then —

She went on through the room in which there had been dancing, in which Bradley Fitch, a little boyish in manner, had announced his plans for marriage. She went through the larger room, where so many had waited the entrance of Naomi Shaw, and through the foyer. She wiped her hands on her apron and opened the door to a slight man in a dark suit, a man with a long, sad face; a man who said, "Is Mr. Fitch in?"

Got a summer cold, Mrs. Hemmins thought, and said, "Expecting you, Mister — ?"

"Wyatt. No. I can't say he is. But — "

"Not even sure he's up," Mrs. Hemmins said. "Hasn't had his breakfast, anyway."

Sam Wyatt snapped fingers on his right hand.

"Didn't think," he said. "Well, I can — "

"Matter of fact," Mrs. Hemmins said, "he's awake, anyway. Somebody came earlier than you. Upstairs."

"Upstairs?" Wyatt said.

"Best way," Mrs. Hemmins said. "Takes in two floors. Another door up there." She indicated with a thumb. "He lives up there, mostly. But come on Mister — what did you say?"

Wyatt said it again. He hesitated, and went in.

60

"Call and see," Mrs. Hemmins said, and went to a telephone and peered at it, and chose a button from among several, and pressed it. She pressed it again, and lifted the receiver.

"Don't answer," she said. "Guess he went out after all. Only — "

She put the receiver back and stood, looking at the telephone as if she expected an explanation from it. Of course, Toby might merely have done something he shouldn't. He often did, and — if apprehended — showed guilt. But the more she thought about it, the more she thought that Toby had acted as if — well, as if someone had frightened him. But if Mr. Bradley wasn't upstairs, nobody was upstairs and — what had Toby been afraid of?

"It's rather important," Wyatt said. "I could try later. But — "

"I'll tell you," Mrs. Hemmins said. "Chance is he's taking a shower. In that glass thing. In there he can't hear goodness, I don't know what he *could* hear. If it's important — *Gesundheit* — I can take you up and show you where — " She hesitated; made up her mind. "Come on," she said. "We may as well find out." She led toward the stairway, and Wyatt went after her.

The door to the second-floor study opened off a hallway, and stood ajar. Mrs. Hemmins rapped on it and said, "Mr. Fitch? Mr. Fitch,

61

sir?" in much the same voice she had used earlier in calling the missing Toby. Behind her, Sam Wyatt sneezed. He's really got a bad one, Mrs. Hemmins thought, and pushed the door open and looked into the study. And screamed.

Bradley Fitch had got out of the chair, but he had not got far — not more than halfway across the room. He had fallen, then. Lying face down on the floor he had vomited again, and then, clutching himself, he had rolled to his side. He had died so.

Everybody leaves New York City over summer weekends. Everybody goes to the beach, or to Long Island or Westchester or nearby Connecticut, or to the New Jersey hills or shore. Subway trains run infrequently; buses hurry along uncrowded avenues; taxi drivers, in considerable numbers, may be found not in the city, but driving on country roads, uneasy to find so much space around them. Except in the theater district, and even there on Sundays, it is often possible to find a place to park a car. (On Sundays, it is less possible to find a place to eat, since the best restaurants do not open.) In the offices of afternoon newspapers a few sit sleepily on Saturdays, or play bridge or poker, since there is no news on summer weekends.

It is true that a few millions remain, for one reason or another. It is true also that some thousands come into town, and may be seen walking dreamily along Fifth Avenue and elsewhere, the men usually in sports shirts and equipped with cameras. There are always some people in New York, even when everybody has left.

It is not usual for Mr. and Mrs. Gerald North to be among them. The Norths have, and for years have had, a weekend place where grass grows — and where Jerry, in adventuresome moments, has sought to make vegetables grow, and Pam flowers. This weekend, however, they were in town, because Jerry had no choice and where Jerry stays Pam, in the ordinary run of things, stays also. Their confinement was due to a man named Braithwaite, who wrote books, who was leaving in a week for Europe, who had got his newest manuscript to North Books, Inc., a month late and who pointed out that if anybody was going to ask for changes — not that he supposed anybody would be so foolish — they had better ask fast. So Jerry, who found he was going to ask for a good many changes, turned typed pages with reasonable steadiness — and wished, rubbing tired eyes, that Braithwaite's typist would remember to change her ribbon occasionally. Pamela read and talked to cats — in low tones, so as not to disturb Jerry. The cats, who hate to be taken to the country in boxes, were evidently gratified by this turn of events.

At five-thirty, Pam, having filled a container with ice, put cocktail glasses in the freezing compartment and sliced lemon peel — and her left index finger, but very slightly — opened Jerry's door and said, "Hey!"

"Why," Jerry said, "can't Braithwaite ever remember what his characters look like? Here on page two hundred and sixty-one he says— "

"I know, dear," Pam said. "It'll be time for cocktails when you've showered. Everything's out."

Jerry looked at her. He said he saw she had sliced the lemon peel. "Oh, that," Pam said. "It's nothing, really. I just put it on to keep the air out. If you don't hurry, we'll miss the news. Even if it isn't Banghart on Saturdays."

Jerry, within reason, hurried. It was five minutes before six when he poured martinis into frosted glasses and twisted lemon peel over them, and caressed the rim of each glass with the bruised peel. In such matters, he is ritualistic. It was precisely at six that he turned on the radio, at six-sixty on his dial, and was promised the news, which would be brought to him by a cigar.

It was not, however, until six-eleven that

the announcer, who was not Mr. Banghart, said, "Now for some names in the news. Bradley Fitch, whose engagement to Naomi Shaw, the star of Broadway's hit play, *Around the Corner*, was just announced, was found dead today in his Park Avenue apartment. Mr. Fitch, who was the only son and heir of the late Cyrus Fitch, was an internationally known polo player. Death apparently was due to natural causes."

"Oh!" Pam said, "how dread — " and was interrupted by Jerry's commanding right hand.

" — has just come in," the announcer was saying, "from the NBC newsroom. The police report the death of Bradley Fitch as suspicious and have started an investigation. The weather and our windup story after these few words about — "

"*Jerry!*" Pam said. "How — *awful*. They were so happy and — oh, *Jerry*." And then Pam began to dab her eyes with the nearest thing available, which happened to be a tiny cocktail napkin.

Jerry moved to her and patted her shoulder and, for want of anything better to say, said, "There. There."

"Such dreadful things happen," Pam North said, and reached up and held to Jerry's hand.

It was much later that Pam said, after a considerable period of abstraction, that, if it had to happen, it was too bad it had happened on Park Avenue.

"Because that's Homicide East, isn't it?" she said. "So Bill won't be in it."

"Nor," Jerry said, and was firm, "will we." But his firmness lessened. "Unless Sam's — " he began, and the apartment bell rang. Jerry went to the door.

Acting Captain William Weigand, Homicide, Manhattan West, looked, to Jerry, a little grave, and also a little puzzled. Sergeant Aloysius Mullins, standing behind Weigand, appeared to be worried.

"Come on in," Jerry said. "You're just in time for — "

"Well," Bill said, "this isn't entirely social. That is — "

He and Mullins came in, and greeted Pam and were greeted by her.

"What it is," Bill Weigand said. "We found a belonging of yours — I'm pretty sure it's yours — in an odd place. And the inspector knows about it, so — "

He produced a small, white square, a little crumpled — a small square of linen. He held it out to Pam.

"Why," Pam said, "it's one of my cocktail napkins. Like this one." She showed another square of white, even more crumpled. "Except I've been crying into this one," Pam said. "See? They both have the 'N' in the corner. And the Siamese cat."

"Yes," Bill said. "I did see that, Pam. How do you suppose it got in Bradley Fitch's apartment? In the room he died in?"

# IV

Pam North said, "In Mr. *Fitch's* apartment?" and then, "They're like match folders, really. Where they are doesn't prove anything."

The three men waited.

"We turn up with matches advertising drive-ins in Nevada," Pam said. "How, we never know. You read about match covers being clues, but how do you explain Nevada?"

"Listen, Pam," Jerry said. "We — "

Pam North agreed her comparison was extreme. But, she said, when they went places, Jerry was as likely as not to put a cocktail napkin in his pocket — "when there are too many things for his hands" — and to forget to take it out and to bring it home. It was sent to the laundry — "if it's not paper, which they usually are" — and in time returned to owners. "If we remember."

"Has Fitch been here?" Bill asked, simply.

"No," Pam said. "We only met him the other night. But — " she stopped.

"It's no use, Pam," Jerry said, and then, to

Weigand, "Sam Wyatt?"

"He was there," Bill said. "This morning. He and the housekeeper found Mr. Fitch — dead. Wyatt was here?"

"Last night," Jerry said. "About this time. Somebody killed Fitch?"

"We don't know yet," Bill said.

"But," Pam said, "it's *Park* Avenue. At least, the radio said it was. And you're always the other side of Fifth."

At the moment, Bill told them, he wasn't. He was working out of Homicide East. It was temporary; it resulted from emergency leaves, added to normal leaves.

"Since we didn't take the napkin there," Jerry said, "and you know we didn't, how about a drink?"

Mullins looked thirstily at Weigand, who hesitated, shrugged. "What Art don't know won't hurt us," Mullins said, and Weigand smiled slightly, said it had been a long day, said, finally, "Why not?" A few minutes later, Pam said, "Now," and, when Weigand hesitated just perceptibly, added, "After all, it's our napkin."

"I'd tell you anyway, I suppose," Bill said. "It's got to be a habit. So far — "

So far, it was merely a suspicious death. It had taken toxicological examination to make it that, although the first physician called — a heart specialist, who had offices in the Park Avenue apartment house — had had his doubts from the beginning. A corrosive poison was an obvious possibility. But so was some violent digestive attack, perhaps resulting from food poisoning. The physician had reported. An ambulance had come, and the police with it, and a medical examiner shortly thereafter. The medical examiner had called it poison, and then it really started. Then Weigand and Mullins came into it, from Homicide East, with the precinct men and, a little later, a team from the District Attorney's Homicide Bureau, with an assistant district attorney. And men from the Police Laboratory. The autopsy was hurried; it was not waited for. By the time the preliminary report came from Bellevue, they were well into it. The preliminary report showed oxalic acid.

"But," Pam said, at that point, "I never thought of that as a poison — not as a real poison." She paused a moment. "I suppose," she said, "because my grandfather used to use it to clean his straw hat. It seems so — domestic."

It was, in a sense, Bill agreed. It was also a poison, and a fairly violent one. Half an ounce would kill; an eighth of an ounce had been known to kill. The amount it had taken to kill Bradley Fitch was not yet determined. Since he had died rather quickly — within, it appeared, not more than half an hour after ingestion — it was probable that the amount taken had been large. He had taken it on an empty stomach; in a concoction apparently intended as a hangover remedy.

And the method of taking was one of the things which cast doubt on the simplest solution, which would have been suicide. Oxalic acid, because it can be procured easily and at small expense (which is not infrequently an item) had once been often used by suicides. In recent years, this had not been so true.

"People don't wear straw hats so much," Pam said, and to this, after a slight start, the others agreed. It might well be that the acid was, as a result of the decline in straw hats, less often readily available in the home.

"People use it for ink stains, though," Mullins said. Weigand looked at him. Mullins said, "O.K., Loot."

A man ready to kill himself would not, it was to be presumed, bother to concoct a hangover remedy, since the cure he planned for other woes would serve for all. The other arguments against suicide were obvious. To all appearances, Fitch had been a man with few troubles and much to anticipate — specifically, marriage to Naomi Shaw. (But appearances, as all know — and as policemen know

71

better than most — are not always trustworthy.)

But further, it appeared that somebody had been with Fitch shortly before (if not actually at the time) he drank the poison. Somebody, at any rate, had rung the bell at the upstairs door. So Mrs. Rose Hemmins testified. He explained Mrs. Hemmins. She had heard the sound of footsteps, and had supposed they were those of Fitch, on his way to open the door.

Weigand interrupted himself there to ask what they knew of the Fitch apartment. "Since you were at this celebration," he added.

They knew, Jerry told him, only a foyer and two rooms, both large, both party rooms.

"And," Pam said, "that the elevator doesn't stop anywhere else, which was most impressive. I mean, when it stops at that floor, of course. You walk right into the apartment, or almost. Instead of a corridor and a lot of doors with letters. Like here."

It was all rather impressive, Bill Weigand agreed. Impressive and a little archaic. He did not suppose that there were now in New York many apartments like the one in which Mr. and Mrs. Cyrus Fitch, emanating the warm glow of great wealth, had installed themselves just before the first world war and ten years or so before the birth of their only child. There had been more such apartments then, and for some years thereafter, but even by the twenties the number had been dwindling.

"Not enough servants any more," Pam said. "Or, I suppose, children either."

Weigand supposed so. It takes a good many servants to staff a duplex apartment of sixteen rooms, several of them disproportionately large. It takes a large family, if people are not to rattle. It takes also, and obviously, a great deal of money, and a corresponding scale of life. "And," Pam pointed out, "not so much living in the country."

Again she was agreed with. So, most such apartments had been cut up into smaller ones. That of the Fitch family had not, although the family, properly speaking, had been reduced to one man. Bradley Fitch had maintained the big place, which occupied a good part of the eighth floor and of the ninth in the twelve-story building. It had entrances on both floors; was internally connected by two stair flights (family and staff) and a dumbwaiter, which had apparently not been used for years. Fitch's own quarters had been on the ninth floor, with other bedrooms and baths; the lower floor was devoted to living areas, a big kitchen, and servants' rooms. Both floors had windows on Park and on the side street — and on a large air shaft.

"So," Bill said, "people who wanted to call on Fitch, and knew their way around, went directly to the ninth floor and he let them in there." Apparently, if the housekeeper was right, somebody had that morning, at eleven or a little before.

"Then you don't know it was Sam," Pam said, and Bill Weigand said they did not, as yet, *know* it was anybody. Certainly, it did not appear to have been Sam Wyatt. Wyatt had showed up half an hour later, and at the downstairs door. He had been let in by the housekeeper, Mrs. Hemmins; with her, he had found Bradley Fitch dead on the floor. It had been he who had gone to a telephone and called a doctor. He had been present still when the police arrived, had told them what he knew, had been asked to wait, in case Homicide had further questions. He had, by choice, waited in the anteroom on which the elevator opened. There, Bill Weigand had talked to him.

It did not appear that he had much of importance to contribute. He had dropped around, on the chance of finding Fitch available. He had been shocked — shocked as Mrs. Hemmins had been — to find what they did find in the upstairs study. He was now more shocked than ever to hear that Fitch had been poisoned.

He had not been asked about the cocktail

napkin, since it had not been found — more precisely, had not been identified — when he was talked to by Weigand and Mullins. The napkin had been picked up in the course of the thorough — the incredibly thorough — examination given a room in which murder has been done. Weigand had identified it as he checked over articles arranged for his viewing. But that had been later.

Wyatt had been asked why he had wanted to talk to Fitch at, for both of them, a comparatively early hour. He had said, at first, "Business," and then, when Weigand and Mullins waited, Mullins' pencil poised over his notebook, Wyatt had amplified. It had been about the play.

"About its closing, of course," Pam said. "We know about that. Sam was here because of that. When he must have picked up the napkin."

It had been about *Around the Corner,* and its closing. Wyatt had explained the situation. He had decided to make, alone and with Fitch alone — "no man's himself with a girl like Nay around," he had explained to Weigand — one more effort to persuade Fitch to be reasonable; to, at least, let Nay remain in the play for another six months. "It seems," Weigand said, "it will make all the difference to a movie sale."

Pam did not see why that would be true; Jerry, after a few moments of thought, said it might. In New York, *Around the Corner* could hardly be more highly thought of. But it had been on Broadway only briefly; there had hardly been time for the rest of the country to hear of it. Motion picture producers, particularly in these days, bid against one another only for those "properties" which were almost universally known. "Like," Jerry said — "oh, like Lindbergh's memoirs." Or, to go back a few years, *Life with Father*. It was when there was bidding that the money rolled in.

In any case, that was the explanation Wyatt had given. He had, he had told Weigand, been moderately hopeful of making Fitch see their point. This hopefulness, it appeared, had arisen during a party Fitch had given the night before at "21."

"One of these damned stag affairs," Wyatt had said, and had snapped his fingers. ("Always do that?" Bill asked. "Most of the time," Jerry said.) Wyatt had dropped in, rather briefly, according to his account. He had had a drink or two. Who had been there? Damned near everybody. Men — theater people — Fitch had met through knowing Naomi Shaw. Other men about whom Wyatt professed to know little. "Probably polo players," he had told Weigand. "People like that." (That he

76

had snapped his fingers then, snapping polo players into oblivion, the Norths did not need to be told.)

Had anything been said, by Fitch presumably, which led Wyatt to think a renewed discussion of the play's fate might be helpful?

Nothing had been said, Wyatt told the questioning police man. ("Very open and aboveboard about the whole thing," Weigand said. "Or seemed to be.") It was — well, it had proved hard to put words to. Fitch had been a good host at the stag party; had seemed a friendly man; even a pleasant man. Wyatt supposed that, subconsciously, he had taken Fitch out of a pigeonhole labeled "Polo Player" or "Rich Man's Little Boy" and looked at him and — liked what he saw. Fitch had been, it appeared, especially friendly with the men from the theater, including Wyatt himself.

"Left me feeling he might have been thinking it over," Wyatt had said. "Hell — left me with the feeling he *could* think. Thought if I got him alone we might work something out."

There had obviously, Wyatt said, been nothing to lose. Or, it had seemed so.

"You don't count on murder," Wyatt said, and snapped his fingers.

"You didn't try the upstairs door?"

"Up — oh, no. Didn't know about it — didn't know Fitch lived up there, as you say

77

he did. I'd only been here once before — to that damned big party."

Had he thought Fitch was drinking a lot at the more recent party — the stag party?

He had not thought so, particularly. Fitch had been all right while he was there. The party was still going when he left.

Did he remember who had been at the stag party? Specifically, by name?

The men in the cast of *Around the Corner*. Strothers, Jasper Tootle. The director of *Around the Corner*, Marvin Goetz. And a lot of polo players. He didn't remember names; he was no good at names. "All pretty much alike, anyway," Wyatt said, contentedly putting them in the pigeonholes, from one of which he had, tentatively, removed Bradley Fitch.

They had let Wyatt go along, after a few more questions. Now they would have to get him back, and ask him about the napkin. There was little doubt what he would say; little doubt what had happened. Wyatt had, absent-mindedly, stuck the cocktail napkin in his pocket while at the Norths'. While with Mrs. Hemmins in the study, with Fitch dead on the floor, he had as absent-mindedly taken it out for some reason. Perhaps to dab with it at a forehead on which, understandably, cold sweat might have formed.

"So this," Weigand said now, dangling the

78

little napkin between his fingers, "won't get us anywhere. Inspector O'Malley thought — well, he thought it might."

"I know," Pam said. "Inspector Artemus O'Malley thought it might get Jerry and me in jail."

(Deputy Chief Inspector Artemus O'Malley, at that time commanding Manhattan detectives, is a conservative policeman, disapproving of amateur intervention — particularly by people named North. He is also somewhat choleric.)

"Well," Mullins said, "we know this much, anyway. It's going to be a screwy one."

And this, also, was because the Norths were in it.

"The elevator man doesn't help?" Jerry asked, and Bill told him there wasn't any. Until noon, the apartment house elevators were self-operating. To get to the ninth floor — to any floor — you got in and pressed a button. To get to the ground floor again, you got in and pressed another button. A policeman's lot, Bill supposed, had been easier before automatic elevators, automatic telephones; easier in Inspector O'Malley's more active days.

"I'd think," Pam North said, "she'd keep a cat."

Sergeant Mullins set his glass down very carefully. He looked at Mrs. North with anxiety evident on his solid face. Jerry was gentle; his words might have been as fragile as eggshells.

"Who, dear?" Jerry said.

"But evidently she doesn't," Pam said.

"Please, Pam," Bill Weigand said.

"Alone so much of the time in that big place," Pam said. "Oh — perhaps a dog, but it would have been the same thing. Mrs. Hemmins, of course."

"Mrs. North," Sergeant Mullins said. He spoke in a hushed tone. "You're saying a cat and a dog are the same thing?"

It didn't matter, Pam said, since obviously it wasn't either. Or, for that matter, a horse.

At that, Jerry said, "Oh." He turned to Weigand. "Actually," he said, "she's talking about Sam Wyatt." He considered this. "In a way," he added.

"He'd have been sniffling," Pam said. "He's very susceptible. He — " She stopped, since Bill was looking at her intently.

"He was," Bill said. "You're saying he's allergic?"

"Why," Pam North said, "of course, Bill. What else would I be saying? He was sniffling? And his eyes were running? When you talked to him?"

"Not a great deal," Bill said. "Slightly. I supposed he had a summer cold."

"For all we know," Jerry said, "he had. He may have caught one last night. Anyway, even if there is a cat — or — "

"Not a horse," Pam said. "Unless — but that's silly."

They waited.

"It just occurred to me," Pam said, "that since Mr. Fitch played polo so much, whatever it is about a horse might have sort of — well, stuck to him. But that would have been other clothes, obviously. It's almost certainly a cat. Mrs. Hemmins sounds exactly like a cat."

"Listen, Pam," Jerry said. "Bill knows Sam was in the apartment. He was in the apartment when Bill talked to him."

"In the anteroom," Pam said. "Where the elevator stops. Not really inside. But he had been." She paused. "Of course," she said. "That's why he was in the anteroom. Probably the cat doesn't get there. What kind of cat is it, Bill?"

"I didn't see any kind," Bill said, and spoke abstractedly. "This allergy Wyatt has — the symptoms come on quickly?"

"He wasn't here five minutes," Pam said. "I thought at first he was — well, crying because the play was closing. Of course, I suppose it would be three times as quick here, wouldn't it? Because of three cats."

The three cats, who find a group of four humans excessive — more than four is impossible — had withdrawn. Being addressed, they appeared, in a body, in a doorway, their tails arching in enquiry. "Good evening, Martini," Bill said, knowing who must be first addressed. "Gin. Sherry." Martini spoke briefly, Gin not at all, Sherry at length. "We're not having any, Sherry," Pam said. "She thinks canapés, because we're having cocktails. Of course, we don't know how many Mrs. Hemmins has. They wouldn't have been around, of course. Too many policemen."

"Look," Mullins said. "We *know* he was in the apartment. He says so. This Hemmins says so. We don't need a cat to prove it." He paused. "Do we?" he said.

"No, sergeant," Bill said. "All the same — " He crossed the room to the telephone, saying, "All right?" to the Norths and getting "Of course," in that exchange dictated by convention, if not by common sense. He consulted a memorandum, dialed a number. He said, "Weigand. Is there a cat there?" He waited a moment. "Yes," he said, "a cat. I don't care what kind of cat. Or, a dog will do, apparently."

He turned, telephone in hand, and raised enquiring eyebrows.

"Oh, that's what Sam said," Pam said. "A

cat is better. That is, I mean worse, of course."

Bill nodded. He said, "Well, ask her, will you? I'll hold on. Oh — and ask her if Mr. Wyatt had a cold while he was in the apartment."

"Thinks I've gone nuts," Bill told the others, while he waited.

"Well," Mullins said, in a tone of consideration. Bill grinned at him. He said, "You say yourself they're always screwy when the Norths — " and broke off, to say, "Yes?" He listened.

"Big black fellow?" he said. "Have the run of the place? Or didn't you ask?"

The policeman who had answered the telephone had, it appeared, put cat and cold together, and come up with an answer — and the proper question of Mrs. Rose Hemmins. The cat did have the run of the apartment; of both floors, except that Mrs. Hemmins tried to keep him downstairs when Fitch was at home. She tried, but that morning she had failed —

"Right," Bill said. "And the cold?"

He listened. He said, "Wait a minute. Is she certain?" and listened again and said, "It may be. Ask her again." He waited. After some little time, he said, "Right," and turned back.

"Mrs. Hemmins says he had a cold," he

said. "But — she says he had it when he arrived."

"Oh," Pam said, "then it was really a — " But she did not finish it.

"Right," he said, when she did not. "Or — he hadn't just arrived. The cat — it's a big black cat, the boys say — had been upstairs. Visiting Fitch, apparently. So — " He shrugged.

"Perhaps he *has* got a cold," Pam said. "Anyway, I know he — " But again she did not finish.

"He took it hard," Jerry said. "The play's closing. Not only because of the money but — writers are odd people, sometimes. He kept saying the play was nothing. Couldn't imagine what people saw in it. All the same, it was — hell, it was a dream come true. And — "

Now it was his turn to hesitate.

"We can't keep it back, Jerry," Pam said. "We've tried before, and we never could. Last night Sam said he wished somebody would — would put poison in Mr. Fitch's soup. Of course he was probably joking but — what did you think, Jerry?"

"Oh," Jerry North said, "sure he was joking — I guess."

Bill Weigand stood for a moment in thought. Then he said, "Better finish your drink, sergeant. We'll go ask Mr. Wyatt how his cold is."

★

They did not find Samuel Wyatt immediately available for enquiry into the condition of his health. He lived in an apartment hotel on the East Side. He was not in his room, nor in the hotel dining room. Mullins was left to sit in the lobby; Weigand went to a small office in the precinct house occupied by Homicide East. He did paper work.

The preliminary report was confirmed by further toxicological examination. Bradley Fitch had died after ingesting between half an ounce and an ounce of oxalic acid, served him in a concoction which had consisted of tomato juice, bitters, and, probably, Worcestershire Sauce. It had contained, also, Tabasco sauce and, apparently, additional red pepper. The preparation, Weigand thought, would disguise the flavor of almost anything. What it would do, even without oxalic acid, to an empty stomach, Weigand preferred not to think. Fitch's stomach had been empty, which had hurried the action of the poison. Death from oxalic acid poisoning had been known to occur in as little as three minutes' time, in the event of hemorrhage. Fitch had hemorrhaged.

The glass from which Fitch had drunk bore no fingerprints but his own. The bottles from which the various ingredients had been taken bore his and Mrs. Hemmins', the latter more numerous. But on the bottles, the prints were slightly smudged; it was possible the containers had been picked up by someone who chose to hold them in a cloth. Evidence of this was, however, and in the opinion of the laboratory man who had initialed the report Bill Weigand read, inadequate for court presentation. They were a long way from that, Bill thought. They were still a considerable distance from proving murder — particularly if no one else had handled the glass.

The possibility there was obvious, and had not been overlooked. Several small metal trays had been found on the counter in the serving pantry. They revealed no fingerprints at all. This might indicate Mrs. Hemmins was thorough as a housekeeper; the other possiblity was preferable. Mr. Fitch had been served his final drink, as he must have been served many others in his thirty-one years of life — properly, on a tray. Whoever had so proffered it had, also, been scrupulous in washing up.

The second-floor doorbell could, as Mrs. Hemmins had said, be heard on the floor below. So could the footsteps of someone moving between the bedroom and the door. (But not in all rooms of the floor below, only near one of the flights of stairs.) When the rooms were checked, the outer door had been found to be unlocked. It was, however, of a type which unlocks automatically when the knob is turned from within, so would have been unlocked after Fitch opened it. (If he did open it.) To lock it after him, a departing guest — or murderer — would have had only to press a button set into the inside knob. This had not been done. What this indicated, if anything, was not clear. Much was not clear.

Fitch had died the possessor of a large, but unappraised, estate. His attorneys declined an estimate. Pressed, they said, "Well, several millions." The money had been made by the late Cyrus Fitch and by the not so late Abner Fitch, father of Cyrus. Bradley Fitch had done little to add to it, which was understandable. Bradley Fitch had not married. He had once before been engaged, and that quite recently. (To one Margaret Latham, daughter of Mr. and Mrs. Arnold Latham, Park Avenue and Easthampton.)

Pending examination of Fitch's will, the identity of his heir or heirs was not established. There were several relatives, but none (it appeared) nearer than cousins. One cousin was Mrs. James Nelson who lived, with her husband, in Rye, New York. Other relatives would be reported as discovered.

Oxalic acid was readily obtainable at any pharmacy. It was used as a bleach by workers in leather, marble and brass. It was used to clean straw hats and remove ink stains. It was used for cleaning bricks. In appearance, it was crystalline and resembled Epsom Salts. It had a bitter taste. There was little point in seeking to determine the source of the crystals used, at least until there was more to go on.

Fitch had got home the night before at some time undetermined, but after two A.M. The night elevator operator, who went off duty at that hour, leaving further ascents and descents to the control of tenants, was pretty certain he had not taken Mr. Fitch up before he left. Fitch had been host at a party at "21" the night before — a party, it appeared, got up more or less on the spur of the moment. The party had not so much ended as dwindled away, seeping, as time went on, from the private room in which it had started to the long bar downstairs, where it had lost identity.

A cat had been in Fitch's bedroom and in his study. The police vacuum cleaner had picked up its long, black hair.

The telephone rang. "He's just come in, Loot-I-mean-captain," Sergeant Mullins reported. It was then a little before nine. Bill Weigand drove the few blocks to the hotel in a Buick convertible with the top down, not looking particularly like a policeman. In the lobby, he joined Mullins, who did. Samuel Wyatt said, "Sure, come on up," on the telephone, and they went on up. Wyatt had a corner suite. He wore a sports shirt and slacks. He said, "Come on in. Something turned up?" They went in.

"One or two points," Bill said. "How's your cold, Mr. Wyatt?"

"Cold?" Wyatt said. "What makes you think I've got a cold, captain?"

"When I talked to you earlier I thought you had," Weigand told him.

Wyatt began to shake his head.

"I don't — " he said, and ended, "oh, *that*."

Bill Weigand nodded. He said, "Right."

"Not a cold," Wyatt said. "Allergy. The housekeeper's got a cat, apparently." He looked at Weigand, and his eyes narrowed and he snapped his fingers. "Is it supposed to prove something?" Wyatt asked, in a slightly different voice. "If so, what? You know I was in the apartment — hell, I was there when you talked to me."

"In the anteroom," Bill said. "Not actually in the apartment, Mr. Wyatt. But you had been, I realize that."

"Hell," Wyatt said. "I found the poor guy, didn't I?"

"These symptoms," Bill said. "They come on quickly, Mr. Wyatt? Within a few minutes?"

"That's right," Wyatt said. "Dropped in on

some friends the other night and I hadn't been there five minutes — " He broke off. He snapped his fingers. "Sure," he said. "The Norths. Friends of yours, aren't they? They started you on this?"

"In a way," Bill said.

"Friends of *mine*," Wyatt said. "Talkative, aren't they?"

"Not particularly," Bill said. "Any reason they shouldn't be? About this?"

"Hell, no," Wyatt said. "Everybody knows me knows about this. Get it from anything on four legs, damned near. No secret."

"Then," Bill said, "these symptoms — what are they, by the way?"

"Runny nose," Wyatt said. "Sneezing. Running eyes. Gets so bad, if I let it, I damned near can't breathe."

"Right," Bill said. "It comes on fast. You went into Mr. Fitch's apartment this morning and almost at once you began to have difficulties?"

"Within a few minutes," Wyatt said. "Doesn't start all at once, of course. What's all this about?"

"In the anteroom," Bill said. "Outside the apartment proper. Where the elevator — "

"I know where you mean," Wyatt said. "Where you asked questions."

"Yes," Bill said. "Where we talked. The

90

symptoms didn't seem so severe, then. Not as you describe them."

"Clears up pretty quick sometimes," Wyatt said. "Also, I'd been waiting around for a while. Cat doesn't get out there, apparently."

"No," Bill said. "Then why, I wonder, Mr. Wyatt, did Mrs. Hemmins think you had a cold — *when she opened the door to let you in?*"

For an instant, Bill thought, Wyatt's eyes went blank. But of this he could not be sure. Then Wyatt's eyes widened, his eye brows went up, his long face was all surprise.

"I don't know why she'd say that," Wyatt said. "Must have got things mixed up. It started after I got inside. Where this cat had been." He snapped his fingers, absently. "Hell," he said, "whatever it is doesn't come through a closed door."

He looked intently at Weigand. He said, "What *are* you getting at, captain?"

"Before you got there," Bill told him, "there was someone on the floor above. With Mr. Fitch. With him when he took poison. Probably gave him the poison. And — the cat had been up there recently, Mr. Wyatt."

There was a longish pause.

"So," Wyatt said then. "Well, *I* hadn't, captain. This missus — what did you say her name was?" Bill told him. "She's got it mixed up."

"Perhaps."

"I'd settle for that," Wyatt told him. "Pretty much have to, won't you? I say one thing. She says another. Doesn't get you anywhere, does it?"

"It raises a question," Bill told him.

"And — I've answered it. I didn't poison the polo player."

"And you weren't on the second floor?"

"Sure I was. I went up with this Mrs. Hemmins and — "

"You know what I mean. Before that."

"No."

The answer was unhesitating.

# V

They had not let it stop there. For more than an hour after Sam Wyatt's unhesitating denial that he had gone alone to the second floor of Fitch's duplex, they had taken him over it. But it could not be argued that they had made perceptible progress.

Wyatt had no convenient proof that he could not have been at the apartment some time before he rang the downstairs doorbell and was let in by Mrs. Hemmins — could not have been in Fitch's study, and Fitch's serving pantry, long enough to have concocted, and served, the "eye-opener" which had permanently closed Bradley Fitch's eyes; could not, with the poison's effect already apparent, have left that floor, gone down in the automatic elevator, got himself readmitted. He said that he had left his apartment and walked the few blocks to the Park Avenue apartment house, that he had gone up immediately and rung immediately, and been let in by Mrs.

93

Hemmins within a few seconds.

But he could not prove this. He had not kept precise track of time. He had not, so far as he knew, been noticed going out and, while this would be checked, checking would hardly help. (It is seldom that anyone says, "Oh, there goes Mr. Jones. It is now precisely ten-eighteen and one half.") He had not, walking that day quiet streets of Manhattan's upper East Side, encountered anyone he knew. He had not seen the doorman at the Park Avenue apartment house. "Probably off getting someone a cab."

Wyatt had been entirely reasonable. He had appeared entirely cooperative. Several times, he expressed regret that he could not be more helpful. Once he said, obviously, that had he known about all this in advance, he would have used a stopwatch. "Except I haven't got one."

He had been equally reasonable about the cocktail napkin with the neat "N" in a corner. He had not, at first, recognized the napkin. Prompted, he had agreed that (if the captain said so) it might well be a belonging of Mr. and Mrs. North, and that he might, absent-mindedly, have put it in his pocket when he left their apartment the evening before. He had done things like that before. This time, he might very easily have done it. "All I was thinking of was getting out of there. *Three cats.*"

He was surprised that the napkin had been found in Fitch's study. He didn't see why he would have left it there. But, again, he had not been precisely calm, precisely himself. "Hell, the poor guy was lying there dead. You walk in on something like that and — " He might have taken the napkin out of his pocket without knowing it, might have dropped it on the floor. It had been on the floor?

"On a table," Bill had told him.

On a table, then. Anywhere. Only — he didn't remember anything about it, one way or another. All he knew was, if it was there, and he had carried it there, he had left it when he had been there with Mrs. Hemmins, when they had found Fitch dead. Because that was the only time he had been there — the only time he had ever been there.

He admitted, he had said, having dinner with the Norths at the Plaza, seeing Fitch come in with that cousin of his — "Woman tried to get me to make a speech at some club" — that it would be all right with him if someone put poison in Fitch's soup. Something like that — whatever the Norths said. He didn't question what they said.

But as for meaning anything like that — *really* meaning anything like that — He had

95

snapped his fingers; he had said, "Oh, come now, captain. What the hell?" People said things like that. They didn't mean them. If they did mean them, they didn't say them. Hadn't Weigand ever said, perhaps about some — oh, some politician he thought a menace — "Too bad somebody doesn't knock off that Joe Whatever's-his-name?" without meaning to suggest the desirability of any such action? Merely as a manner of speaking?

"No," Bill had said, to that.

Well, a good many people did. Perhaps the captain was an exception. Reasonable he should be, in his business.

"Fitch irritated me," Wyatt had said. "I don't deny that. The whole thing irritated me. It was all so damned pointless. So damned — well, I guess arrogant is the word. And, I lose what's to me a lot of money. Because some spoiled polo boy — " He stopped. "Keep forgetting the poor guy's dead," he said. "Anyway — that's all it was. I was just sore. I'd had a couple of drinks. Let it show. It didn't mean — that!" He snapped his fingers, snapping it off.

For all the finger snapping, Wyatt had been calm, been reasonable, throughout. There was only, to raise doubt, that instant when his eyes had gone blank. Or, had they gone blank? Bill Weigand could not be sure. He drummed his fingers lightly on the desk at which he sat, in his temporary office of the Homicide Squad, Manhattan East.

"For my money," Mullins said, "he's lying."

"For your money he killed Fitch?"

Mullins hesitated a moment. Then he said, "I guess so. He's covering up. So — " He stopped. "We've not got a lot to hang it on," he said. "Cats. And whether a guy had a cold before or after." Mullins shook his head. He said it would be nice, sometime, to have a good pro kill.

They couldn't, Bill said, a little absently, have everything. They —

The telephone rang. Bill answered, identified himself. He said, "Why, yes," and, after another moment, "Right." He hung up. "As soon as I can."

"The girl," he said. "Miss Shaw. Wants to see somebody. She sounded frightened."

Gerald North became, dimly, conscious that something was amiss. From the depths of sleep, from the stillness and the darkness of the depths, he bobbed to the surface and floated there restlessly, half in sleep and half out of it. There were recurrent waves, on which he bobbed. A wind was rustling in something and something creaked in the

97

wind. He was a fish and his native habitat was water but now he was in the air, and he gulped for the water which he breathed and —

"Oh, dear," Pam said. "Oh, dear."

"Guh-sleep," Jerry said, still largely asleep himself.

"Tossing and turning," Pam said, and this time it was more clear. "*And* twisting."

"Guh —" Jerry began, and said, loudly and excitedly, "What's the matter! What —"

"Oh, dear," Pam said. "I didn't mean to."

Jerry sat up in bed. He looked at the neighboring bed, and there was enough light for him to see Pamela. She was not tossing and turning, but lying very quietly on her back, looking at the ceiling. She had, however, thrown back the sheet and summer blanket, no doubt during the process of twisting. The short nightgowns she had recently adopted were, Jerry thought — now no longer dimly — most becoming.

"I really tried not to," Pam said, and turned to look at him. "I know how you hate to be waked up."

"Well," Jerry said. "No more than most people."

"Oh," Pam said, "I'm sure, much more. Although, of course, I don't wake up other people much. I thought you were never going to. That is, for all I was trying not to, I —"

She paused. She sat up in bed. "All right," she said. "I got very lonely. All this to worry about, and no one to help."

Jerry switched on the light between the beds.

"I still don't understand why you don't get cold," Pam said.

"The difference," Jerry told her, and looked at her, and was not wide awake, "is immaterial." He looked again. "Singularly," he added. "Do you want a cigarette?"

"A cigarette would be fine," Pam said. "We forgot the stocky man. And we practically sicked Bill on poor Mr. Wyatt."

Jerry sat on the edge of his bed to light Pam's cigarette, and then his own. He sat back on the bed, leaning against the pillow.

"What stocky man?" he said.

"The one we forgot to tell Bill about, of course."

"The — " Jerry began, in a tone of enforced quiet. "Oh, the one at the bar?"

"And at the party," Pam said. "The one who stalked. The one with Miss Shaw. And — the very night before somebody killed Mr. Fitch. Don't you *see?*"

"No," Jerry said. "He was her cousin."

"It was," Pam said, "hardly worthwhile waking you up. Her cousin, indeed!"

"Well," Jerry said. "Somebody said he was."

"Might be. But that was before Mr. Fitch was poisoned. Which makes all the difference."

"Look," Jerry said, and ran a hand through his hair. "What difference? If he was her cousin before — I mean — that is." He took a deep breath. "It wouldn't de-cousin anybody," he said.

"On the whole," Pam said, "I guess I didn't wake you up very much, did I? Lying here worrying, all by myself — deserted — and I make a few little sounds — very small sounds, really — just on the chance and now all you do is talk about people being de-cousined." She sighed. "You may as well go back to sleep," she said. "I'll do it myself."

"What?"

"What I just said — worry."

"Why not in the morning?"

"Because," Pam said, "it isn't the sort of thing you can put off. Anyway it's keeping me awake. Listen — will you just listen?"

Jerry would.

If he would, he was told, he would see the situation. It was one they had to face. Sam Wyatt had come to them — well, come to Jerry — to be sustained. Had come trustingly. And what had they done? They had told about his allergy, which otherwise the police might never have heard of —

100

"Oh," Jerry said at that point, "come now, Pam."

Might not, then, have heard of so soon. But the point was, it had been heard of from them. And, as a result of that, there had been the discovery of Mrs. Hemmins' cat and then Mrs. Hemmins' assertion that Wyatt had had symptoms *before* he entered the apartment. Or — before he was *supposed* to have entered the apartment. And, as if that were not enough, they had told about the poison in the soup.

"Probably," Pam said, "he's in jail this very minute. And we just sit here."

"If he lied about being in the apartment before," Jerry said, "probably jail's where he belongs."

"There might be a hundred explanations of that," Pam said. "The point is — what about the stocky man?" She paused. She stubbed out her cigarette in an ash tray. (It continued to smolder; Jerry reached over and stubbed further. For this, absently, he was thanked.) "*Jerry!*" Pam said. "You know — what if they were in it together? A — a beaver game."

"Beaver?" Jerry said. "Oh, badger."

"Let's not argue about animals," Pam said. "Mightn't it?"

Jerry drew deeply on his cigarette.

"I don't quite see — " he began, and did

not finish, because, when he began to look, he did see. It was a long jump, they had nothing to jump from. There were several possible landing places. Still —

"This is one thing I've thought about," Pam said. "Lying here, unable to sleep, with nobody to — "

"All right, darling," Jerry said. "You were put upon. What thing?"

"Naomi Shaw and this — this cousin," Pam said. "I don't suppose he'd actually be a cousin, of course. She gets herself engaged to a man with all this money and — oh, I know — gets him to make a will leaving it all to her. Not as Mrs. Bradley Fitch, of course. As Naomi Shaw. And then she and this man kill Fitch and they whack up."

"Look," Jerry said, "if she's that kind of girl — and I must say she doesn't look it — why wouldn't she just marry Fitch? Why get involved in murder? And, as you say, 'whacking up' the swag?"

"Because — " Pam said. "For one thing, I don't know what you mean she doesn't look it. Just because she's so pretty. Show me a man who can — "

"Subject," Jerry said. "Subject, Pamela."

"All right," Pam said. "You brought it up. Suppose she's already married to this man and — *Jerry!*"

They had been talking in low tones, as became the hour, the possibility of sleeping neighbors. At his name, so spoken, Jerry jumped slightly against the pillow.

"That's *it!*" Pam said. "Don't you remember? She *was* married. Somebody — oh, Sam Wyatt — told us that. She comes from Kansas City and probably it was somebody there, and he comes out of the past and has a hold on her and — and — you know about Kansas City. Gangsters."

She was, Jerry told her, slandering a considerable city. However —

"You make it lurid," he told her.

"I don't," Pam said, "argue that I've dotted every 't.' But — it's certainly much more likely than Sam Wyatt. After all, he's a writer. And writers just — think about things. Except Hemingway, who shoots things. And he's an exception."

In many ways, Jerry agreed.

"Well," Pam said, "don't we have to tell Bill about this — gangster? About his meeting Naomi Shaw where they wouldn't be seen? To plot the murder?"

"In other words, possibly. But — yes. Tomorrow."

"And Sam Wyatt in jail?" Pam said.

In the end, Jerry did telephone. Acting Captain Weigand was gone for the night.

103

"If we went — " Pam said, but Jerry, this time, was firm, and Pamela was acquiescent. She said, "All right, tomorrow," and turned on her side, and breathed deeply twice, and slept like a kitten.

Jerry tossed and turned. He twisted. He got himself a drink of water and he smoked another cigarette. Finally, he returned to the Braithwaite manuscript which had kept them for the weekend in New York. Then Gerald North slept quickly.

Two weeks after *Around the Corner* opened, Naomi Shaw, who had started as a featured player — with Sidney Castle — had become a star. "Critic's Darling Elevated to Stardom," the *Daily Mirror* reported. A week after that, she had rented herself a little house — a very little house, she had told her friends, and had added, "But of course I'm not very big," and this her friends, particularly when male, had found charming. (It is true that Jane Lamont, Naomi's understudy, had remarked that she couldn't see that darling Naomi was so damned little as all that. "You'd think," Jane had said, "that everybody else was big as an elephant." But even Jane Lamont had been, to a degree, tolerant, as even women often were of Naomi Shaw.)

The little house was squeezed between

larger houses on a residential street of the upper East Side. It was a three-story house, but it was not much more than twenty feet wide. One climbed to the door, up a flight of stone steps, with an areaway below. One walked into a small foyer, and on the left could enter, from it, another small room with a single window and a large cabinet which contained radio and television and a record player. That it was difficult to sit far enough from the television, which had a large screen, was really (looked at properly) the more fun.

Beyond these two rooms, reached by a doorway from the foyer, was the living room, which occupied the width of the house and was almost forty feet long, and had a far end of glass. Beyond the glass was a "garden," occupied by a tree. In a near corner there was a narrow staircase leading up, and in the far corner, on the right, there was another leading down — down, as it happened, to the kitchen, and through the kitchen, to the garden.

It was a charming little house, even from the outside, where Bill Weigand stood at eleven forty-five Saturday night. He was alone.

There was a light in the single small window next to the door; there was a light, dimmer, visible through the glass of the door. Bill Weigand pressed a button and there were soft chimes within. He waited, and nothing happened, and he pressed the button once more. He waited longer, and pressed again. It was still some seconds before he was answered. Then Naomi Shaw came to the door herself. She looked first through the glass, and then opened the door until a chain held it. She said, in a soft voice — in the voice which no one had ever quite described — "Who is it?" The voice seemed meant for better words. Even these, they caressed.

Bill Weigand told her, and she said, "Oh," and hesitated. She said, "It's so late, isn't it?" but then, "What an odd thing for me to say."

"You telephoned me," Bill told her.

"Yes," she said. "Yes, of course."

Then she released the chain and said, softly, "Come in, please," and Bill went in. She led him through the foyer and down the living room, and there turned.

Five feet three, Bill thought — but thought subconsciously, in an official corner of his mind. Weight about a hundred and five. Brown hair, worn rather long; very large brown eyes, set rather far apart. Face, what is known as heart-shaped; mouth, rather full-lipped. Wearing —

She *is* damned lovely, Bill Weigand thought, in an unofficial corner of his mind.

— wearing a fitted black thing — house coat, belted. Very covering, very severe. Made of some heavy stuff — silk, he supposed.

Actually, Bill thought, she stands as if she didn't weigh anything at all. It wouldn't make any difference if she wore a — a mother hubbard.

She was pale, except that her lips were bright. She put a hand to her broad, white forehead and lifted the heavy dark hair from it and pushed it back a little, and she moved her hand and the hair fell where it had been. The gesture was slow; as she raised her arm the sleeve of the house coat fell back to her elbow, and the line of forearm and wrist and hand was a perfect line.

"I'd almost forgotten," she said. "I'm — I'm so very tired." There was the little check in her voice. The same, Bill thought, that she used at the end of the second act. But now, as then, the check — the fleeting hesitation — was right — exquisitely right. She was too tired — but not quite too tired — to remember words.

"Of course," he said. "I wouldn't have bothered you. But you telephoned."

"I know," she said. "We must sit down, mustn't we? Please?"

She indicated a chair, and again the gesture was beautiful. She sat on a sofa.

"It's all been like a dream," she said. "A dreadful dream but — not a nightmare. Everything a little smudged. It's all seemed so — unreal." Again she lifted the heavy hair from her forehead, and again released it. "I haven't even cried," she said. "Why, do you suppose?"

"It happens that way," Bill said, and waited. She looked at him, as if, still, it were his turn to speak. "You said, after I told you I was one of the men investigating — " He hesitated. "Mr. Fitch's death," he said. "You said, 'I have to tell you something. Tonight. Can you come to my house?' "

"Did I?" she said. "Yes, I must have. I'd fallen asleep, I think. Yes, I know I had. I waked up and — everything was very clear. You know how it is, sometimes? Like a bright light? But then — little by little there isn't any light? I suppose it's all part of a dream, don't you? The afterglow of a dream?"

"I don't know," Bill said. "You had something to tell me?"

"That's just it," she said. "I — thought I had. It was all so clear. I had to do something about it right away, so I telephoned you, but then — you must understand how it is. Can't you? Can't you even try?"

She leaned a little toward him, sat so that, leaning forward, she lifted her chin as she looked at him. Damn it all, Bill thought. It's completely real. But — in the play she does that. When — when is it? In the third act? But that is when she's making up the story about her father. Of course —

"I'll try," Bill said. "But you're not really telling me you called about a dream?"

She shook her head slightly, and said that it was not as simple as that. She said that many things were not as simple as we tried to make them — as words made them. "But I'm not very good at words," she said. "Somebody else writes the words for me." He would have to be patient. She had been ever since she had — had heard — in this almost numbed condition. She did not know the right word for that. Probably it was what they called shock. Then, that evening, after she had eaten something — "and I had a drink before; two drinks" — she had gone to sleep. Or, she said, into a kind of half sleep.

She had wakened from the sleep, or half sleep, suddenly — so suddenly that the awakening was itself a kind of shock. And in that instant of waking, and even for some minutes afterward — "long enough for me to call you" — it had seemed to her that what had happened was very clear, very certain.

"It must have happened to you," she said. "Surely it must happen to everybody. That feeling of — illumination? I suppose, actually, it's because, although you think you're awake, you're not really awake. I know Sam told me once — " She paused. "Mr. Wyatt," she said. "He wrote my play."

"Yes," Bill said.

She looked at him intently. She was, he thought, trying to find something in his face. He began to doubt that she would find what she wanted to find.

"Mr. Wyatt told me," she said, and the intentness was in her softly lovely voice, "that he dreams plots sometimes. Stories, you know? And that when he first wakes up they still seem good — oh, sometimes for as long as half an hour. And then — then, he said, they fall apart in his hands. They weren't really anything to begin with. This was like that. As if I'd made up a story while I was asleep. And — "

Suddenly, she covered her face with her hands. Her body trembled under the house coat. Bill was tempted to touch a slender, shaking shoulder, and did not. She raised her face, after a moment, and her eyes were dry. "I can't cry," she said. "Why can't I cry? It's as if — inside — I still don't — don't believe that Brad's — that Brad's not alive."

Weigand shook his head. He waited a moment. He said, "What was this — story, Miss Shaw? A theory about Mr. Fitch's death?"

110

"He was killed, wasn't he?" she said. "It was that?"

"Yes."

"Everybody's been so — so careful about it," she said. "People called up and wanted to come around and — I only wanted to be alone. Phyllis — she's in my play, you know — did come but — but after a while she saw I'd rather be alone. She was so sweet — but — Somebody tricked him into taking this poison?"

"Apparently. You had a theory? When you waked up this evening?"

"Yes," she said. "That was it. Only, it was the way I said. It — it fell apart in my hands. After I called you."

"Why? You thought of something that didn't fit?"

"I suppose so. But, really, because none of it fitted. I called back at your office, but they said you'd already gone out."

"What was the theory, Miss Shaw?"

"No," she said, "it wouldn't be fair. Now that I know it — it can't really be right."

Nevertheless, he told her, they were interested in any theory. In any possibility. It took him a little time. She seemed very reluctant. Once — he thought to gain time — she interrupted something she was saying and listened, and then she said she thought she had

111

heard something; and then that, probably, she had only heard Nellie, and that Nellie — Nellie Blythe — was her maid, and had a room on the third floor.

"If there's nothing to it, nobody will be hurt," he told her, several times, in several ways. He was asked, finally, if he promised that. He promised that. Then —

Putting it in words, she said, made it the more absurd. Arnold Latham, Jr., had been furious. Perhaps that wasn't the word. He had been bitter. That was true. Strangely, disproportionately bitter.

About what?

But she thought everybody knew. Brad had been planning to marry Peggy Latham. Arnold's sister. A date had even been set.

"And then Brad and I met," she said. "We — neither of us could help it. Brad felt awful about Miss Latham but — what could he do? It would have been worse to go on with it and — it wouldn't have been fair to anybody, would it? But Arnold couldn't see it that way. He — he said dreadful things to Brad."

"Mr. Fitch told you this?"

"Yes."

"Mr. Latham said threatening things?"

"I don't know if they were really threatening. Just — very angry things. You see, the Lathams haven't — well, they haven't too

112

much money. Not the way people like that have money. I suppose — but that would be a dreadful thing to say, wouldn't it?"

"That Mr. Latham was counting on his sister's marrying a very rich man? Was disappointed enough to kill because of that?"

"I told you it was wrong," she said. "It was just — something happened to my mind."

"So far as you know, Mr. Fitch hadn't — " He hesitated. "Miss Latham isn't expecting a child by him?"

She straightened at that, opened her large eyes very wide.

"People like that?" she said. "But really, captain! That sort of thing doesn't happen to them."

Only to poor little working girls, her tone implied.

The others — what did she think? That they knew too much? The files of almost any adoption agency, if she could look at them — which she could not — would tell her a different story.

"So far as you know, Mr. Fitch hasn't left her money? As — as a sort of compensation?"

"Why," she said, "he wouldn't have done *that*. That would be — such a crude thing to do."

"Yes," Bill said. "Very crude, Miss Shaw. You know Mr. Latham, Jr.? His sister?"

She had met Arnold Latham once or twice, before she and Fitch had — made up their minds. Peggy Latham, she thought, only once. "A blond girl, quite tall. The kind who plays golf."

"Did Mr. Latham seem to be a violent person?"

"No. I told you it was all — that it wasn't right. You made me tell you about it."

"Yes," Bill said. "I did. When you were formulating this theory, Miss Shaw. Didn't it occur to you that, if Mr. Latham was going to kill anyone, it wouldn't be Mr. Fitch?"

She looked at him. She appeared to be puzzled.

"I don't — " she said, and then shook her head. The heavy, dark brown hair swayed with her head's movement.

"You," Bill said. "If anyone. That's obvious, isn't it? On the assumption that, with you out of the way, his sister would be back in the money? Literally, in the money?"

"I didn't — " she said. "What a — a frightening — "

"Miss Shaw," Bill Weigand said, "why did you ask me to come here?"

She had an expressive face — for all its dainty beauty, a very expressive face. They had told Mary Shaftlich that, years ago, when she was taking elocution at Northeast High

School. Her face was, now, extremely expressive. Words were unnecessary. She's really good, Bill Weigand thought. But it's true she's better when someone else writes the words.

"You didn't ask me to come here to tell me this," Bill said. "You were frightened when you called — frightened and entirely wide awake. Not because of this — this nebulous theory. This — "

"I don't understand," she said. "It's all true. About Mr. Latham. His sister. It's — "

"Right," Bill said. "Say it's all true. Or — say there's truth in it. Why did you want me here?"

"Because — "

"What happened between the time you called me and the time you came to the door and let me in? To make you give this very excellent — performance?"

"I don't perform," she said. "I'm an *actress*. Anyway — "

A man laughed. The laughter was brief, it was heavy, it was more derisive than amused. Bill Weigand whirled in his chair; his right hand made an instinctive movement toward the revolver which New York policemen are required to carry at all times. Bill saw the man's legs, first, as the man came down the narrow flight of stairs in the corner of the long

115

room. Then he saw the man — a man of medium height, a rather stocky man. The man's hands were in full view.

The man reached the foot of the staircase and started toward them. After a few steps, he said, "I've seen you better, Mary."

She was on her feet. The movement was quick, lithe, for all its haste, infinitely graceful.

"*You!*" she said. "Don't call me that."

"All right, Mary," the man said. "I'll call you Naomi. You still didn't get very far, did you? All that trouble for nothing."

"You spoiled it," she said. The beauty was still in the voice. "You — you spoil everything." The little hesitancy, the little catch, was there. "You always did. Always — always — always."

She formed two slender, graceful hands into tight fists, and shook them, both together, at the stocky man. At which, he laughed again.

# VI

## *Sunday, 12:20* A.M. *to 4:20* P.M.

The stocky man's laughter was brief. It seemed to Bill Weigand that, this time, there was amusement in it.

"Act one, scene two," the man said. "Impotent rage. Or — is it petulance, my dear?"

"Get out of here," Naomi Shaw said. "Just get out of here." Her voice went up somewhat. It was still a lovely voice, but it was not quite the same voice. There was, Bill thought, suddenly a trace of Missouri in it — the merest trace of Missouri.

"Pear-shaped tones, Mary," the man said. "Where are the pear-shaped tones?" He seemed suddenly to remember Bill's presence. "For two years," he said. "Almost two years, I heard about pear-shaped tones. You know what they are?"

Bill had heard the term.

"Never could visualize it," the man said. "Not that she doesn't talk right nice. Don't you think she does?"

"Sometimes," the girl said, "I could kill

117

you, Bob. Sometimes I don't know why I didn't."

"Now, honey," the man said, "I didn't give you a chance, remember? Anyway, you aren't big enough. Don't you remember what a little girl you are?" He smiled, then, and the smile momentarily broke the squareness of his face. "And," he said, "you didn't want to, honey. You never will want to." He turned to Weigand. "She was stringing you along," he said. "But I guess you got that, didn't you?"

"Yes," Bill said.

"Matter of fact," the man said, "I thought she was pretty good, didn't you? Not convincing, maybe. But, hell, she didn't have much time. And, like she said, nobody wrote the words for her." He nodded his noticeably square head. "Pretty good act."

"You always do things like this," Naomi Shaw said. "Always. *Always.*" But, now, her voice was softly down again; now the accents of Missouri were smoothed out of it. Naomi Shaw went a few steps, seemed to flow the few steps, and sat in the corner of a sofa. "He always did," she said, to Bill.

"Suppose," Bill Weigand said, "we make this a little less private. For one thing, who are you?"

"Name's Carr," the stocky man said. "Robert Carr, construction engineer. The lady's ex."

118

"Not enough," Naomi said. "Not enough by half."

"Talks British, don't she?" Carr said. "Not arf she don't. Gets ideas in her pretty head, too. Don't you, honey?"

"A year and eight months," Naomi said. "The longest year and eight months ever."

"That's right," Carr said. "Gave me the best year and eight months of her life, the lady did. But Chile — nope. Not for Mary Shaftlich Carr. Not Chile."

"He's not fair," Naomi said to Bill. "He's never fair. And, there's no secret I changed my name. Everybody does."

"You have to get used to that sort of thing," Carr said. "Everybody's in the theater. You know that, captain? So everybody changes his name. Or her name."

"Suppose," Bill said, and his tone was mild, but it was a policeman's tone. "Suppose we shorten this, shall we? Miss Shaw tells me this theory about a man named Latham. Tells it, and at the same time throws it down. You listen. Sit on the top step?"

"Thereabouts," Carr said.

"Until I indicate I'm not buying the story," Bill said. "Then you come down."

"And," Carr said, "you start to reach for your gun."

"Right," Bill said. "It's just as well you

119

didn't. Have you got a gun, by the way?"

"Me?" Carr said. "You're as bad as the lady, captain. Same things, probably. She acts melodrama. You probably run into it. Why the hell should I tote a gun?"

"I don't," Naomi said. "I'm a comedienne. Even in Timbuktu you ought to have heard that."

"Pakistan," Carr said. "You know, in Pakistan you miss some of the most important news, honey. About girls from Kansas City getting to be stars on Broadway. Backward place, Pakistan."

"I'm sure," Naomi said. "You'll fix that. Fill it all full of dams."

"You played a gangster's moll in *Second Precinct*," Carr said. "Got shot for a second-act curtain. Before that you were a maid in *This Mortal Coil*. You screamed in that one. Didn't get shot. All very comic."

"Oh, God," Naomi Shaw said. "Always. *Always!*"

"I said, suppose we cut this," Bill reminded them. "Miss Shaw gets me here to listen to this — this afterglow of a dream. You, Carr, listen to see how it goes over. When it doesn't go over, you come down and start this — whatever it is. Now — you let me in on it. Right? And — *now.*"

"I — " Naomi said.

120

"You," Bill said, and pointed at Carr. "You rest that pretty voice, Miss Shaw."

"Why — " she said, and Bill looked at her. "Oh," Naomi Shaw said.

"O.K.," Carr said. "She got it into her head I killed Fitch. Then she got it out of her head — or I got it out. But she'd already telephoned you, so she could turn me in. Then — "

"That isn't it at all," Naomi said. "I wasn't — "

"Miss Shaw," Bill said, "will you try to keep quiet? For five minutes?"

"Won't do you any good," Carr told him. "Used to say that myself and — "

"And," Bill said, "will you skip all that, Carr? She thought you'd killed Fitch?"

"Said she did. Thought I got jealous, after all these years. If I couldn't have her, nobody could have her. Gets things like that out of these plays she acts in."

Bill looked at Naomi Shaw, and just in time. She closed her lovely lips with exaggerated care.

"Well," Bill said, "were you jealous?"

And then Carr hesitated. He looked at Naomi Shaw, and she looked at him, through wide dark eyes.

"All right," Carr said. "She gets under your skin. Also, she didn't love that polo player. Just kidded herself. Wouldn't have — "

"I suppose," Naomi Shaw said, "I really love you?"

And Carr looked at her for some seconds and then, quite slowly, in a tone almost matter of fact, said, "Yes. You can't get away from it." Naomi said, "Oh, God," in a voice dripping with hopelessness. Carr turned back at once to Bill Weigand.

"She got this idea," he said. "She called me up at my hotel, just as I was turning in. She was — well, pretty upset. She told you she hadn't been able to cry, but she was crying then, all right. Kept saying I'd killed him and that they'd find out — they'd be sure to find out. Meant you people. I told her, hell, I hadn't killed anybody — not for a long time, anyway. Not since the war. If then. Seabees didn't kill people much. But — I couldn't get her to listen. Finally, I said I'd come around and talk sense to her and she said no, I mustn't. So — "

So, he said, he had come, and been let in, and found out that Naomi had already called the police. Because, she had told him, she was hysterical, was frightened. Frightened, he had gathered, of him. He'd have thought she would have had better sense. Although, thinking it over now, he didn't know why he had thought that. She was always the impulsive type. Had been since she was a kid.

"You convinced her you hadn't killed Fitch?"

Carr seemed surprised at the question. He said, "Sure." He added, "That was the easy part."

"Convince me," Bill Weigand told him.

That would be easy, too. Fitch was killed this morning. Carr looked at his watch. Yesterday morning. Carr hadn't been in town. He had been in Chicago. "That's where the company headquarters are," he said. "People I work for." Told this, Naomi realized how absurd her suspicion was. "You see," Carr said, "she thought I was still in town."

"Still," Bill said. "Then you had been?"

Carr had come to New York from Chicago, getting in on the Century Thursday morning. Did Weigand want to know why he had come? Weigand nodded. He had come on business; to see a man about a dam. A dam in South America, this time. "We build a lot of dams," Carr said. He had conferred, with the first man and then with others, until late Thursday evening, and had had dinner, and then decided to see "my old girl friend," before he went back to Chicago. It had been almost midnight; he had gone to the hotel; found that Naomi was not at home, and had talked to her maid. The maid had told him about "this big party."

"So," Carr said, "I took a chance and called Snaith. You know Snaith?"

"No," Bill said.

"Flesh peddler," Carr said. "That the right term, honey?"

"Always," Naomi said. "But *always*. Mr. Snaith is an artists' representative."

"Caught him just as he was leaving," Carr said. "Said how about taking me to this shindig and he said, sure, why not. I met him there and he took me in. Although, far as I could see, anybody could've walked in. We were in time for the big scene. 'Going to steal your girl — ' "

"That's like you," Naomi said. "Exactly like you."

"O.K. Let's say I'm sorry," Carr told her. "Anyway, it seemed like a good time to get out of there. I got out of there."

"Like a little boy with the sulks," Naomi told him. "Oh, I saw you."

He had been tied up the next day, and into the next evening. He had taken a late plane back to Chicago; had, early in the afternoon, read of Fitch's death and had flown back to New York. He had telephoned Naomi at once, but he had got only the maid, who had said that Miss Shaw was not talking to anyone. He had tried persuasion, and got nowhere. "I never got anywhere with these maids of yours," he said, to Naomi. "You know that. They seem to think I'm bad for you."

"Why shouldn't they?" Naomi asked.

"O.K.," Carr said. "Anyhow, I said I was in town, and where I was, and asked this biddy to condescend enough to tell Miss Shaw that her former husband had called, and would help in any way he could."

"How?" Naomi asked.

Carr paid no attention to that. He said apparently the biddy had condescended, since his former wife had called him up. "To accuse me of murder," he said.

"I came over here," he said, "and, like I told you, convinced her I didn't poison Fitch. Then she said she had called the police because — because she was afraid. I said — "

"You said a lot of things," Naomi Shaw cut in.

"All right," he said. "I was sore. You could always make me sore. Got a lot of fun out of it. Then I said, all right, we'd both wait until the police came and she could tell her story and I'd tell mine. And then she got this notion. This notion about not wanting to drag me into it. Anyway, that's what she said. Said to leave it to her. About then, you rang the bell." He paused and looked at Naomi, and away from her. "Probably just wanted to give this performance," he said. "The part about keeping me

125

out of it — " He shrugged.

"That's right," she said. "Don't give me any credit. That's right. Just another chance to show off."

"I'd rather have it the other way," he said. "You know that." He waited a moment. She said nothing. "So I listened," he said to Weigand. "I thought, actually, it was pretty damn good. Red herring, but not too red. But — you didn't buy it, so I decided there was no use in letting her get in any deeper, specially when I didn't have anything to worry about, so — " He paused for a moment. "Well," he said, "that's the size of it. We've wasted your time."

"Right," Bill said. "If you can prove you were in Chicago. You've wasted a lot of time."

"Oh," Carr said, "I can prove that." He spoke with confidence. Weigand looked away from him, looked at the girl on the sofa. Naomi Shaw was looking with an odd intentness at her former husband. It was, Bill Weigand thought, as if she were waiting for him to say more; almost as if she were willing him to say more.

"No trouble about that," Carr said, and did not look at Naomi.

"Until then, you believed them?" Pam North said.

The Weigands and the Norths were having breakfast in the Norths' apartment, although it was somewhat after Sunday noon. It was not to be called "brunch," because Pam wished it not to be called brunch. She said it made it sound like such a noisy meal. They had had strawberries and then eggs benedict, which Jerry prepared, it being an established thing that Pam could not make hollandaise, that it always separated.

"I thought they were probably telling the truth," Bill said. "Even now — " He lighted a cigarette, and said yes to hot coffee.

"Why?" Dorian asked him. Bill looked thoughtfully at his wife, whose eyes were greenish, who had moved with her coffee to a sofa and sat with one long leg tucked under her, and so made a lap for the cat named Sherry — and often, because of the way she clung to laps, referred to as "The Limpet." "Since," Dorian said, "it doesn't sound too terribly probable. I mean, the whole feel of it."

That, Bill told her, was precisely it. Granted that, retold — of necessity summarized, since he had, finally, been with Carr and Naomi Shaw in her apartment for almost two hours — the interview seemed theatrical, even concocted. But — at the time, it had not felt that way. At least, not until Naomi Shaw

127

had looked with such intensity, such an air of expectation, at her former husband. Grant, further, that she had play-acted, and Carr had played along — still, what Dorian called "the feel of it" had been authentic. Part of the feeling, Bill said, was that they had never got over each other; that when they were together there were special currents between them. And that, he thought, they did not act. He was not, further, at all convinced that Carr had acted at any time. Also, he said, Carr had had a reservation on a late plane to Chicago Friday night, and he had had one on a plane back Saturday afternoon. He granted that such matters could be arranged.

"By a stand-in," Pam suggested.

That would, certainly, be the most simple way. Although it might also prove to be the most risky way. But they had no evidence about that, one way or another. They would get it.

"It was merely," Pam said, "that all at once you had a hunch they'd left something out? Something important. Even before Jerry and I told you?"

"Yes," Bill said. "That she expected him to tell more than he did. Or was afraid that he would. It looks, now, as if what he didn't tell about was this meeting you and Wyatt saw."

"If Fitch did leave her money," Jerry said.

"If she and Carr were in cahoots."

It appeared he had left her money. At least, he had told her he was leaving her money. Weigand had asked about that, and Carr had stared at him coldly, and Weigand had been unaffected by the stare. Fitch had told his fiancée that he planned to change his will. That had been several weeks before. A few days later he had told her that he had changed his will. So, at any rate, Naomi Shaw had told Weigand.

"I didn't want him to," Naomi Shaw had said. "I said money wasn't the point at all and we were going to get married so soon, anyway."

Fitch had laughed at that, according to Naomi Shaw. He had told her she was no businesswoman; had, lightly, told her she would, now, have to learn to be. He had explained. As things stood — had stood — the money would go to relatives — relatives all right enough in their way, but only that. After he and Naomi actually were married, the law would insure her dower rights. But, there remained an interval — an interval in which something might happen. (Would not, of course. Still might, of course.) "He — he said he might fall off a horse. He laughed about it."

She had not, she told Bill Weigand, really

understood why it was so important. That, she thought, had surprised Bradley Fitch. He had been, for one of the few times she had known him, painstakingly serious. There was a great deal of money. He had not made it. But he was responsible to it. He had said it so — responsible *to* the money. He had — this Bill Weigand gathered from what the girl said — to see that, even if only for a few weeks or days, the money was taken care of. So, he had made a new will. After they were married, he would make another will, in which Naomi Shaw, known also as Mary Shaftlich, and as Mary Shaftlich Carr, would be more simply designated as "my wife, Naomi Shaftlich Fitch." Things would be kept in order.

He had not told her the exact provisions of this interim will. Whether he had told his relatives of it, she did not know. The only relative he saw much of was a cousin, Alicia Nelson. Perhaps he had told her. Captain Weigand should find that easy enough to discover. He had agreed.

But, so far, Mrs. Nelson had not been interviewed. She and her husband were not at their home in Rye. They were away for the weekend.

"Um-m," Pam North said to that and, on being looked at and waited for, said, "Just um-m."

How many other relatives there were, and the closeness of other relationships, they did not yet know. They would, undoubtedly, find out.

"Like dragon's teeth," Pam North said. "All coming up in surrogate's court."

"Like — ?" Jerry said and then, "Oh. Of course."

At the time Fitch was killed, around eleven o'clock Saturday morning, Naomi was, she said, having breakfast. Her maid could vouch for that. She had heard of his death a little after noon, from Wesley Strothers. "He was so — so sweet," Naomi said. "I suppose I should have insisted on playing the matinee, at least, but he just wouldn't have it."

"Strothers called again, while I was there," Bill told the Norths and Dorian.

Bill had been standing to leave; Carr, after a questioning look at Naomi, had said, "O.K. But I'll be around," and stood also. Then the telephone rang. Naomi Shaw flowed across the room to it, hesitated a moment, said, "Yes?" and then, "Oh, yes, Wes." She spoke very softly, the hesitancy — the hesitancy which had defied so many descriptions — was evident. Her voice was sad — much sadder than it had been when she talked to her former husband, to Bill Weigand.

"Oh, Wes," she said, after she had listened

for several seconds. "I don't know, Wes. It's all so — so new — so hard to — " She had not finished. She had listened again. In the same sad, soft voice she had said she *did* understand. She *did* appreciate. She listened again and said, "Oh — I couldn't. Not *next* week," and again stood, gracefully, the fingers of her free hand just touching a table top, and listened. "Perhaps," she said, then. "Perhaps, Wes. I — I may as well, mayn't I? Now that it's all — all — " It appeared she ran out of words at that. She listened again. "All right," she said. "Monday, then," and then, after a brief pause, "You're very sweet, Wes." She replaced the receiver, gently. She stood for some seconds, looking down at the telephone. She turned from it, and it was, Bill said, as if she had reached a decision. She had looked at Bill Weigand and at the browned, square man who had been her husband, and it was as if she hardly saw, or did not clearly remember, them.

But after another few seconds she said, "Oh. Wes Strothers. He has to know, of course."

"The show must go on," Carr had said, and Bill Weigand had expected the duel between them to be renewed. But the girl had merely, tiredly, shaken her lovely head, not in negation, but in, Bill thought, weary acceptance

132

— acceptance of cliché, and of fact. She had looked, not at Carr, but at Weigand, and had said, "Haven't you finished, now?"

Bill had, for that place, that time. He went, and took Carr with him. But he had finished with Carr, also, for the time. He dropped Carr at Carr's hotel on lower Fifth Avenue.

"So," Dorian said, "she's going to go on in *Around the Corner?*"

So, Bill told her, he gathered from what she had said to the play's producer. It would, Pam North said, please Sam Wyatt. It would please a good many people — in time, a good many thousands of people.

"I may as well say it," Pam North said. "It's an ill wind. Will she get a lot of money, Bill?"

There was a lot of money, Bill told her. Enough so that even a part of it would be a lot. Enough so that, if Mary Shaftlich continued to be Naomi Shaw, it would be because acting was more than a means to livelihood.

"It is," Dorian said. "Everything she does proves it. All she did last night."

The telephone rang. The call was for Bill, and Dorian said, as much to the cat called Sherry as to anyone, that it never failed. "Never," Dorian said. "Never." She stroked the long, delicate bone — the seemingly so fragile bone — of the little cat's slender jaw.

133

Sherry purred, more or less in her sleep.

"Right," Bill said into the telephone. "I'll go around and see." He hung up, with that.

"It's never been known to fail," Dorian said again, this time to her husband.

"The cousin," Bill said. "Mrs. Nelson. Has something to tell us."

"I suppose," Dorian said, "in Rye?"

Mrs. Nelson was not in Rye. She was at the Barclay. So, it might not be too long.

"I'll be here," Dorian said. "If they'll have me. Or at home."

Bill kissed the top of her head. He went. "Why I ever married a policeman," Dorian said. She was told, by Pamela North, that she knew perfectly well. "Oh — that," Dorian Weigand said, and scratched Sherry behind the right ear. But then Sherry spoke in a querulous voice, and at once dropped to the floor, where she stretched, rather elaborately, and scratched behind the same ear. "You're an ungrateful cat," Dorian told her. "Anyway my foot was asleep."

She stood up and also stretched, less elaborately but with almost equal grace.

They had another cup of coffee around and Jerry went to commune with Mr. Braithwaite, who could never remember, from one page to the next, what his characters looked like; who had, too often for comfort, made the forgetful authors' category in *The New Yorker*.

"It's too bad," Pam said, "we didn't bring our sewing. Publishers are as bad as policemen."

They could, Dorian supposed, but in the tone of one who supposes nothing of the kind, go to a movie. They did not. Instead, Dorian sketched cats and Pam, luxuriating in it, did part of a crossword puzzle, until stumped by the one-time skipper of the *Golden Hind*. After that, she watched Dorian's quick pencil — and thought of murder.

At a little after four the telephone rang again. Dorian looked up quickly, with hope. But Jerry answered in his study, and did not call, so it was not Bill. Jerry came out, instead.

"Wyatt again," he said. "Apparently he wants his hand held. I suppose we'd better." He appeared pleased.

"He seems to have a very lonely hand," Pam said. "If he's as dull as he must be, I don't see why you publish him."

"Sam?" Jerry said. "He's not — "

"Not Sam," Pam told him. "Mr. Braithwaite, of course. Anybody can see anything's better than reading him."

"Oh," Jerry said, and was not quite guilty. "Braithwaite is adored by thousands. Get your bonnets."

Dorian, evidently included, hesitated. There was, she said, a chance — perhaps one in a hundred — that Bill would finish with Fitch's cousin, would telephone.

"Oh," Pam said, "he'll know you're somewhere."

Since there was no questioning this, Dorian Weigand tied up her drawing pad. They went to the cocktail lounge in which they last had held Samuel Wyatt's hand. Wyatt was there, and snapped fingers at them. His eyes brightened on observing Dorian, as was the custom of male eyes. But it was evident he was morose.

# VII
## Sunday, 4:20 P.M. to 6:15 P.M.

They sat in one of several semi-circular alcoves, on a curving banquette. Sam Wyatt snapped his fingers and a waiter came; Wyatt made it clear that he was host. But, with the orders given and the waiter gone, Wyatt drew invisible designs on the table top with the forefinger of his left hand, while absently snapping the thumb and middle finger of his right. In these activities, he seemed engrossed; seemed, indeed, to have forgotten that he had applied for hand holding. Watching his nervous hands, Pam North thought they should be held — by someone.

"*The Last Mile*," Wyatt said, suddenly. "That was the title." He now looked at the Norths, at Dorian Weigand. "That's what it was, all right." They looked blank. "Guy goes to the electric chair," he said. "Cell to little door — the last mile." He looked from one to the other. "God," he said.

The waiter brought drinks. Wyatt looked at him, as if without recognition, with set face.

137

"First it's months," he said, and looked at his drink as if he could not imagine its purpose. "Then it's weeks and the appeal's denied, and the governor won't act, and you keep on hoping. You know there's nothing to hope for, but you keep on hoping. Then it's hours, and you think, 'It's not yet — not next minute or the minute after. It's really a long time.' But then it's only an hour and then half an hour and then you hear them coming. The floor's cement and their feet make a gritty sound and they come past one cell and past another cell and then — then they stop. And then they put the key in the lock and it's the greatest harshest sound ears ever heard and then — "

Wyatt stopped speaking. He shuddered. He seized his drink and half emptied it. He put it down and clutched the table edge with both hands.

"You hang on to something," Wyatt said. "The bed, maybe. They have to drag you away and you grab hold of the bars and they break your hold and then you're out in the space between the cells and all the others are looking at you from theirs and — " Again he stopped. And now he looked again at the others. He snapped his fingers.

"Imagination is a curse," he said, in quite another voice. "What'll you all have to drink?"

They looked at their glasses, which no one had touched. "Oh," Wyatt said. "You've got drinks, haven't you?"

He shrugged, jerkily.

"Me," he said, "I'm scared. They'll railroad me." He looked, angrily, at Jerry North. "You know damned well they will," he said. "The man who finds the body."

"They won't railroad you," Jerry said. "Quit writing it, Sam. Save it for the novel."

"Novel?" Wyatt said, encountering a new word, an unexplained word. "Novel?" He snapped his fingers. "Oh," he said. "That. That's out for now, Jerry. What would I do with any more money? Just pay it to the government." He paused again. "Anyway," he said, "the last book I did brought me — what? You're the publisher."

"Not much," Jerry said. "But — by the author of *Around the Corner*. That'll make a difference. Even if it is closed."

"Closed?" Wyatt said. "It'll run for years."

"Then Bill was right," Pam said. "He thought she would."

"Bill?" Wyatt said. "Who's Bill?"

They told him. To the name, Dorian added, so that there would be no misunderstanding, "My husband." Wyatt looked from North to North.

"Whose side are you on?" he asked them.

"That's all I want to know."

"Nobody's," Pam said. "That is — Bill's, of course. But yours too. If it's possible."

He looked at her with care. He snapped his fingers. He said, "I've got nothing to hide," with great emphasis.

"The play," Jerry said. "What about the play?"

"Close for a week," Wyatt said. "Nay gets over this polo player." He paused. "Do it in a day, myself," he said. "But she's a girl. Reopen a week from tomorrow, she smiles through her tears, show goes on. Runs two hundred more performances. Maybe they'll close one night. Be a nice gesture. 'There will be no performance of *Around the Corner* tomorrow night, in honor of the author's electrocution.' "

"Come off it," Jerry said. "The play's set, then?"

"So Wes Strothers thinks. Talked to Nay last night. She as good as agreed, he said. And — why not? No more polo player. May as well go on being an actress. It's an ill wind."

"That," Pam told him, "is precisely what I said."

"Well," Wyatt said. "Did you? What we all need is a drink."

Jerry agreed to that; Pam and Dorian did not, on the assumption it would be a long time until dinner.

"Mr. Wyatt," Dorian said, "why do you say you'll be railroaded?"

"Handiest," Wyatt said. "I found him." He paused. "The poor guy," he said.

It was no reason, Dorian told him. He must have an odd idea of the way the police worked. Merely the finding of a body — Dorian's tone properly diminished that.

"Mrs. Weigand," Wyatt said. "You seem a very nice girl. You're a very good-looking girl. Where's your mind? I'm making eighteen hundred a week, less ten per cent. This polo player's going to spoil it. So, why shouldn't I spoil the polo player?" He shook his head; he snapped his fingers. "Don't think this husband of yours hasn't thought of that," he said.

"All right, Mr. Wyatt," Dorian said. "Have it your way, then. You killed Mr. Fitch to keep the play going."

"Now you've got it," Wyatt said, with approval. "Knew a girl with green eyes would be bright under the surface." He looked at her closely. "You know," he said, "they *are* green, or damned near. Very uncommon thing, green eyes."

"Really," Dorian said. "Did you kill Mr. Fitch? Because my husband would like to know." She paused. "I think," she said, "that I will change my mind about another drink, Mr. Wyatt."

"Thought you would," Wyatt said, and snapped fingers for a waiter. "Have to tell you, though. I didn't kill the polo player. Just pushed open a door and there — " Sam Wyatt stopped.

"I thought," Pamela North said, in the sudden silence, "that it was the housekeeper — Mrs. Lemmings — who opened the door."

"Hemmins," Wyatt said. "Lemmings are rats or something. Try to swim oceans. Get drowned. She did, as a matter of fact. The other was just a way of speaking."

"Because," Pam said, "she would be the one, of course. It was her house, in a way."

"I told you," Wyatt said. "She did. I'd never been at the place before, except once, at this party. Not like Wes, who was there half his time."

He snapped his fingers. They waited. He addressed his remarks to his almost empty glass, looking up from it only now and then.

"Had to shop around for money," Wyatt said. "Wes, I mean. A thousand here, two hundred there."

"Yes," Pam said.

"Takes a lot of money," Wyatt said. "They say it's stagehands. Ever notice how it's always somebody like stagehands?" Nobody said anything, and Wyatt, after a considerable pause, asked where he was. He was told. He continued, speaking in small jerks.

Someone had introduced Strothers to Fitch. Fitch had glittered in Strothers' searching eyes; he had appeared likely to exude money. In the end, he had. Wyatt did not know how much, but it had been enough. In the course of the campaign, Naomi Shaw had been "dangled."

"Kind of a door prize," Wyatt said. "Know how it is. Put up the money and meet the pretty lady. Enticement to angels. Nay is, as a matter of fact. All on a very high level. Worked out that way. Worked out that way too damned much, as it turned out. Here was Fitch all ready to marry somebody else — lady polo player from what I heard — and he meets Nay and — " Snapped fingers substituted for a word.

"The one she told Bill about," Pam said and Wyatt looked at her blankly. "You remember," Pam said, to Jerry. "Miss Shaw told Bill in the — the make-believe. A Miss Somebody."

"I'm damned," Wyatt said, "if I know what you're talking about."

"Latham," Pam said. "A Peggy Latham. I didn't know she played polo."

"Oh," Wyatt said. "Way of speaking. Probably doesn't. Rides to the hounds or something. Comes to the same thing."

"Not for foxes," Dorian Weigand said.

Wyatt regarded her, as blankly as he had regarded Pam. He shrugged, jerkily. Anyway —

Anyway, Fitch had dropped the lady polo player. Just as he had dropped somebody *for* the lady polo player. "All," Wyatt said, "on a very high level." He snapped his fingers. "Phyllis," he said. "That's how it went. Phyllis introduced Wes to Fitch, and Wes introduced Fitch to Nay." He looked at them. Now they looked blankly back. "Phyllis Barnscott," he said. "Girl in my play. Very nice girl, as blondes go. Knew her way around. Where was I?"

"I," Jerry North said, "am damned if I know, Sam." He looked at the others. "Does anybody know where Sam was?" he asked.

"He started," Dorian said, "with Mr. Strothers, who, I take it, is the producer, and Mr. Fitch. With Mr. Strothers' having been at Mr. Fitch's half his time."

Wyatt snapped his fingers. He looked at Dorian Weigand with admiration.

"Knew I started somewhere," he said. "Well, that's all I was saying. Wes and Fitch got pal-sy. Each one a new breed of cats to the other. Broadway. Meadow Brook. The twain meeting. Wes told me about it — about — " He stopped. He said everybody needed an-

144

other drink; when the others did not, had one himself. He said he was doing all the talking. And at that, suddenly, he smiled and his face changed entirely.

"As a matter of fact," he said, "that's what I wanted, probably. Somebody to talk to. I've been wandering around. Making up stories about being in the electric chair. Very realistic stories. Got to feeling, hell, I had to talk to somebody. Wake myself up from — nightmares."

In that instant, he was very serious.

"Also," he said, "I thought you two — I didn't expect Mrs. Weigand — could — well, fill me in on what to expect. Since you're in with the cops. Do I walk out of here into handcuffs?"

"I don't think anybody does, yet," Pam said. "There are — there seem to be a good many people. A Mr. Carr. And Mrs. Nelson, of course."

"The woman who wanted me to make a speech," Wyatt said, and looked around the room with what appeared to be apprehension. "Does she get the money?"

"We don't know," Jerry said, and spoke firmly. "Do we, Pam?"

"Of course not," Pam North said. "How could we?"

"Probably does," Wyatt said. "She's some

kind of relative, she says. A cousin, or something." He snapped his fingers. "Funny thing," he said, "the polo player called everybody cousin. Funny how people fall into habits like that." He snapped his fingers. "Makes them think they're different." He brightened. "Maybe they'll pick this Nelson gal."

"You know," Dorian said, "you have the strangest ideas, Mr. Wyatt. Do you really think the police just — 'pick' one person out of a crowd? Say, 'I'll take that one'?"

"For all I know," Wyatt said. "What about Carr? You mean the Carr was married to Nay? How did he get into it? I thought he was in Persia or somewhere."

"Pakistan," Pam said. "Only now he's in New York. Except that at the right time he was in Chicago."

"Probably just an alibi," Wyatt said. "Probably right here, feeding the polo player arsenic."

"Oxalic acid," Jerry said.

"Comes to the same thing," Wyatt said. "But have it your way." He paused, sipped his new drink. "You know," he said, "this relieves my mind. Carr. This woman who wants me to make a speech." He snapped his fingers. "The lady polo player," he said, with evident pleasure. "No fury like. Spurned love

146

turns to hate. You are a cad, and here is a beaker of cyanide of potassium."

"It doesn't," Pam said, "sound much like a lady polo player."

"Oh," Wyatt said, "just a rough draft. We can clean up the dialogue. She had a brother, too. The lady polo player. Maybe he got around to avenging her honor. Or — " He paused. "Losing money makes people touchy," he said. "If I had a sister set to marry a few millions I'd get touchy about it if it — walked away." But then, his mood changed again. "However you look at it," he said, "I found him. That's what they go by."

"I can't," Dorian Weigand said, "think what it is you read, Mr. Wyatt. Or — are these just things you write?"

"You know," Wyatt said. "You're quite a girl. It's too bad you're married to this policeman."

"Listen, Sam," Jerry said. "I know you like to talk. Just listen. As I understand it, you and this housekeeper — Mrs. Lem — *Hemmins* — found Fitch's body. You and she went upstairs together, she knocked on the door, opened it when there was no answer, and you both found Fitch dead. Was that the way it was?"

"Sure," Wyatt said. "We saw he was dead, and she was pretty much knocked out and I went downstairs and called a doctor. She told me who to call. Man had an office in the building. Then I went back. Told this Bill of yours how it was."

"Yes," Jerry said. "But — you keep leaving Mrs. Hemmins out of it."

"Don't know why," Wyatt said. "She was there, all right. I suppose — " He hesitated. "I suppose I dramatize it," he said. "Habit forming, dramatization."

"Mrs. Hemmins," Pam North said slowly, "says you had a cold — she thought it was a cold — *before* she let you in. But if it was cats, not a cold, then — "

"Mrs. Hemmins got it wrong," Wyatt said. "I had that out with Captain Weigand. I was perfectly all right until I got into the apartment, where the cat was." He looked at Pam, then at Jerry and Dorian. His eyes were a little narrowed. "That's the way it was," he said.

And then he pushed his glass back. There was decisiveness in the movement. "If nobody wants another?" he said, and, at almost the same instant, beckoned the nearest waiter, asked — rather abruptly — for a check. There was, unexpectedly, a certain awkwardness in the few moments of waiting for change; in the time it took Wyatt to select a bill and coins for a tip. It was evident that Sam Wyatt had got his talking done.

But, when they all stood to leave, he seemed to sense this and said, with less than his customary abruptness, that he had almost forgotten he had an appointment. The others made polite sounds to this, further polite sounds in payment for their drinks.

Outside, since they declined to be "dropped somewhere," they watched Sam Wyatt get into a cab. And, as the cab drew away from the curb, they watched a sedan, of no particular appearance, start up from a little way down the block and fall in behind the cab.

"I think," Pam North said, "that maybe Mr. Wyatt is right to be scared."

Mr. and Mrs. James Nelson occupied a suite at the Barclay. Acting Captain William Weigand, temporarily of Homicide East, was invited up, and went up. He was received by Mrs. Nelson, who was slim in a black dress, who had short gray hair, who met Weigand at the door. She said it was so good of him to come. She said that she was so sorry her husband had had to step out. She enquired, after she had said, "Please, sit down, captain," whether she could not get him something. She said, "They're so very prompt here. Such an excellent hotel."

Bill was not in need of anything. He was

149

inspected, not obviously, but he thought thoroughly, through attentive brown eyes. He waited for it. Alicia Nelson smiled. "Really," she said, "you're not quite what I expected."

That, Bill Weigand had heard before. To that, he had never thought of a responsive answer. He smiled, instead.

"I am so glad," Alicia Nelson said, "that it is somebody like you. I'm sure we speak the same language."

Bill was not. He did not say he was not. He made a rejoinder which was vague and, he hoped, encouraging. He decided that Mrs. Nelson's black dress, in style and material — how interested women always were in material, and in what they called "detail" — would please Dorian, who was not easily pleased. He thought it had been chosen with care, and without regard for cost. He thought that a suite at the Barclay, presumably for a weekend, would run high.

"Are you sure I can't have them bring something?" Mrs. Nelson said. "If only a cup of tea?"

"Quite sure," Bill said, remembering he spoke the same language.

"And you're really in charge of the investigation into poor Brad's death?" she said.

Bill told her how that was. Deputy Chief Inspector Artemus O'Malley was in charge.

He himself was — well, active.

"O'Malley," Mrs. Nelson said. "Oh."

"You have," Bill said, "some information to give us?"

"Really," she said, "I'm not sure. We felt — my husband and I, that is — that somebody would want to confer with us. Since we happen to be in town — but only until tomorrow — we felt it would be convenient if we talked here. For everyone. At home there are so many things to do, you know." She interrupted herself to smile. She smiled very briefly. "The club takes so *much* of my time," she said. "And James, of course — " But she did not end by saying anything about the demand on James's time. Instead, she said that her husband would be so sorry to miss Captain Weigand.

"Now," she said, "how can we help, captain? Help your investigation of this shocking, shocking thing?"

"If I knew the answer to that — " Bill said, and shrugged just perceptibly. He trusted he was speaking the right language. It appeared, however, that he was not. Mrs. Nelson looked at him, evincing no great comprehension. "We haven't really got far enough to know what questions to ask," Bill told her.

"But, surely," Mrs. Nelson said. "It's been more than twenty-four hours. I supposed

151

that, in that time, the police would — well, have theories, at least. Perhaps already be quite sure, only lack proof."

So that was it, Bill thought, and found the thought interesting. Summoned not to be informed, but to inform. He said that, as to theories — He said there were, obviously, certain possibilities. He said, "Have you a theory yourself, Mrs. Nelson?"

"James and I have been thinking and thinking," Mrs. Nelson said. "Everybody was so *fond* of Brad. He was such a dear boy. Not as experienced as he might have been, I'm afraid. Taken in by people. But a dear boy."

"Taken in?" Bill said.

"I'm afraid so," Mrs. Nelson said. "Both James and I felt he *was* being, so often. A man — a *nice* man — with so much money — You must know how it is, captain."

He was readmitted to the language league. He nodded his head. He asked if she had anything specific in mind.

"Not really," she told him. "Captain — I really *need* a cup of tea. Or even a cocktail. This has all been a strain, of course. We were so fond of poor, dear Brad. Won't you change your mind?"

Bill permitted himself to change his mind. He permitted himself to accept the offer of a cocktail. Mrs. Nelson used the telephone. She

152

said she so loved the Barclay. She said it had such great dignity, but at the same time so much comfort. She said that, so often, one did not find the two combined. She said that James would be so *sorry* to miss the captain. One does not, Bill decided, discuss the significant if the arrival of a serving person is imminent.

The serving person arrived. He brought a glass jug, embedded in ice. Two cocktail glasses were upended in the ice. The drinks were very cold. The serving person thanked them and departed.

"Only," Mrs. Nelson said, "I find theater people so *difficult* to understand. As I am sure you must."

Bill Weigand was tempted to tell her that some of his best friends were theater people. He refrained. He sipped his drink, and nodded, which might approve the drink or accept Mrs. Nelson's views.

"For a boy like poor Brad," she said. "Just a boy, really. Brought up so differently, of course. Good schools, and all that. And then to be *plunged* into this — this *superficial* life."

When Alicia Nelson saw a word in passage, she pounced on it.

"Plunged?" Bill said. "Was he, Mrs. Nelson?"

"First this other actress," she said. "Then

Mr. — what is his name? Strothers?" Bill nodded. "To get him to invest money, of course. But I'm afraid Brad was *impressed*. Really *impressed*. Because people like Mr. Strothers are so different, of course. So much more — in a way, worldly. You do know what I mean, don't you? 'Twenty-one' and all that. Chi-chi."

The term was one Bill thought had been retired years before. But he nodded again.

"And," Mrs. Nelson said, "they *are* attractive, in a way. One has to admit that. This first young woman — so vivacious."

"Miss Shaw?" Bill said, and was looked at in surprise.

"Of course not," Alicia Nelson said. "The first one. Phyllis something."

"Barnscott? The girl in the play?"

"Girl? Well, I suppose one might call her that. A — youngish woman, at any rate. Pretty, of course. But, in such a *showy* way, don't you think?"

Bill had not yet met Miss Barnscott.

By this, Mrs. Nelson appeared greatly surprised. She supposed of course — She broke off. Of course, the captain knew his own business best. But she would have thought. In view of — everything. Bill waited, thinking this might be another thing he had been summoned for. He sipped the excellent martini.

He was rewarded.

Not that Mrs. Nelson meant to suggest anything, put any ideas in the captain's head. But he *had* asked if she and James had any theories. They had, of course, been unable to avoid thinking of this — this "girl."

She knew, Bill decided, precisely where she wanted to go. She knew how she wanted to get there. He drank very slowly — and noticed that she did not drink at all. Her eyes remained attentive to his face, which did not noticeably respond.

Phyllis Barnscott had, Mrs. Nelson said, been the first of the theater people to cross the path of Bradley Fitch, so well brought up, so essentially innocent. And, of course, so rich. How the paths had crossed, Mrs. Nelson did not pretend to know. What poor dear Brad had seen in her — that she could not pretend to understand. "But I've barely met her and, anyway, it's so difficult to see what *men* see." It was evident that he had seen enough.

"They went *everywhere* together for — oh, months," she said, and the emphasis on the word "everywhere" was special, was almost a little lingering. "I mean, the places they *would* go. You can imagine how poor dear Peggy must have felt." She paused, then. "Peggy Latham," she said. "Such a quiet girl. So — different. Interested in such different things.

155

Horses and dogs, you know."

"Yes," Bill said. "He was engaged to Miss Latham, I understand? When he met Miss Barnscott?"

"Oh," she said. "Even after that. When he was — well, I'm afraid there's no word but 'infatuated.' But Peggy was so understanding. Such an understanding girl. She still expected Brad to — come back to her. Everybody did, of course. I mean, that is, all of us did. What Miss Barnscott expected — well, it's so hard to tell about people like that, isn't it? Even if you know them. Perhaps a great deal. And then to be simply *dropped* for Miss Shaw. To have to stand there and hear poor Brad announce that he was going to marry Miss Shaw. When everybody *knew* what they'd been to each other."

She looked at Bill Weigand expectantly.

"A woman like that," she said. "Without background. Without the *basic* things. The basic *certainties*. To be humiliated, before all her friends. Who can tell what she might do? And — I'm afraid — she knew her way around poor Brad's apartment. Far *too* well. Where he kept things and — " She paused. "Surely you must have thought of the possibility."

"There are a great many possibilities," Bill told her. "You must realize that. Miss Latham was equally — humiliated, I'd imagine. Not so publicly, perhaps, but —"

"*Peggy?*" Mrs. Nelson said. "A girl like *Peggy?*"

"I don't know Miss Latham," Weigand told her. "Or Miss Barnscott."

"Obviously not," Mrs. Nelson said. "Obviously. To suggest that a girl like Peggy Latham, brought up as she's been. With her background."

"As I said, I don't know her. No doubt you're right. You mentioned Mr. Fitch's money, Mrs. Nelson. Hinted various people were — attracted by it." (He hoped he was still speaking the same language.) "As a relative, you probably know who will inherit?"

"Oh," she said, "several of us. But — I suppose since I'm the closest —" She let it go at that, delicately. "Of course," she added, "Brad didn't confide in us about his will. Still, it's obvious, isn't it? Since he didn't live to marry this Miss Shaw? Assuming he really planned to."

She smiled then, and shook her head, as at a naughty boy.

"I hope," she said, "you're not getting ideas, captain? Ridiculous ideas?"

"We have to think of everything," Bill said, temperately. "If he had married Miss Shaw, and *then* died, things would have been different for his relatives."

She ceased smiling. Her face expressed astonishment; what Bill took to be hauteur. She said, now in a cold voice, now not to a naughty boy, *"Really!"* It was clear to Bill that he was speaking another language.

"I'm afraid, captain," she said, "that you don't really understand people like us."

"I told you," Bill said, "that there are several possibilities. You must realize we have to consider all of them. However farfetched."

"Certain people don't do certain things," Mrs. Nelson said firmly, but it appeared that she was somewhat mollified. "I'm sure you realize that, Captain Weigand. And, of course, it isn't as if any of us were — differently situated."

Meaning, Bill decided, "needed the money." He said, "Of course. I realize that." He said, "You didn't know Miss Barnscott, you say?"

"Barely," Mrs. Nelson said. "Such different circles, even when she was so much with poor Brad. I'd met her — oh, months ago. And then at this dreadful party the poor dear boy gave. Such odd people. She seemed to be with a man named Tootle, of all things. But there — one mustn't be intolerant."

"It takes all kinds," Bill told her, gravely. She looked, momentarily, as if there were great doubt of this. She said, "That's very true, isn't it?"

"The night before Mr. Fitch — died," Bill said. "You had dinner with him?"

She looked momentarily surprised, even doubtful. Then she made that sound, with tongue and teeth, which laments the regrettable — in this case, it was to be presumed, the death of Bradley Fitch.

"He was so *gay*," she said. "So — *elated*. He was such a *boy*, captain."

"Was there any particular purpose in the dinner?"

"Purpose?" she said. "We were cousins, captain. We saw too little of each other. My husband had a business engagement and — what could be more natural? What do you mean by 'purpose'?"

"Sometimes," Bill said, "there are family matters to take up. When someone plans a change in his way of living. As Mr. Fitch did."

"I'm sure," she said, "that I can't imagine what you mean."

"Or," Bill said, "feeling as you apparently did that this marriage was — undesirable — you might have — "

"Really," she said. "Really! To imagine that I — "

The sound of a key in a lock stopped her. The door from the hotel corridor opened and a short, fat man entered — a short, fat man in his middle sixties; a red-faced man whose eyes were a little shiny. He wore a blue suit, with vest. There was a spot on the right lapel of his jacket. He took off a hard straw hat and, seeing it, Bill thought how few such hats one still saw. He looked at Weigand and then, quickly, apologetically, at Mrs. Nelson.

"Oh," he said, "back too — " His voice was a little querulous. It was not allowed to continue.

"James," Mrs. Nelson said. "I'm so *glad* you could get back. This is Captain Weigand. The police captain, you know. About poor dear Brad. I've been telling him about our theory. That is — not a *theory*, really. Just something — "

"Policeman," James Nelson said, in his querulous voice. "Theory, m'dear?"

"Of course," she said. "About Miss Barnscott."

"Barnscott?" he said. "Don't — oh, *Barns*-cott. Pretty girl, inspector."

"You're tired, dear," James Nelson's wife said. "He *will* work too hard," she said. "Even on Sunday. You must go lie down, dear."

James Nelson put his hard straw hat carefully on a small round table. The black ribbon which circled it was slightly rusty. Although, Bill thought, it's only June.

"Think I'll lie down," James Nelson said.

"You take care of the inspector, Allie. Pleasure, inspector."

He walked across the large, square room and through the door to the bedroom. He closed the door behind him. He was most careful, Bill Weigand thought, to walk steadily.

Mrs. Nelson had stood when her husband entered. She remained standing. She said, "It was so good of you to come," in the tone which means it is time for you to go. Bill went.

He stopped at the desk. Mr. and Mrs. James Nelson had checked in on Thursday evening. He saw an assistant manager. Mr. and Mrs. James Nelson were not frequent guests at the hotel. It did not appear, in fact, that the Barclay had previously had the pleasure of entertaining them.

Mrs. Nelson was so very chic; her husband — Bill considered. It was hard to put a finger on. But Mr. James Nelson did, somehow, seem a little seedy. He was also, of course, a little drunk; it was likely that he was often a little drunk. He wore a hard straw hat. Pam, Bill thought, would be interested to hear of that.

He found a telephone. He talked to Mullins. The man who had been keeping Sam Wyatt under observation had let him get away. Wyatt had met some people for drinks at a hotel on lower Fifth Avenue. He had taken a cab from there to his hotel. He had remained at the hotel for half an hour or so and left on foot. He had walked to a subway station, and ridden to Grand Central. He had been lost in Grand Central.

"One man, Loot," Mullins said. "You know how it is. Probably noticed he was being tailed and — *ffut!*"

"I doubt if it matters," Bill said.

"The people he had drinks with," Mullins said. "Guess who they were, Loot."

"Mr. and Mrs. North," Bill said. "And Mrs. Weigand, probably."

"The trouble with you," Mullins said, "is you're clairient."

"Absolutely," Bill said. "Find out what you can about a man named Nelson — James Nelson. Lives in Rye. Middle sixties, probably. Husband of Fitch's cousin."

"O.K., Loo — captain," Mullins said. "He figures?"

"Well," Bill said, "he wears a straw hat."

He hung up. He made another call.

# VIII

Gerald North sat between Pam, on his left, and Dorian Weigand, in the semi-darkness of a movie house on Eighth Street. The screen in front of them was occupied by an enormous face, which expressed anguish. Gerald North knew it was anguish because the face had, a moment before, been parted from its love, which was as large a face. When last seen, the other face had been wearing an expression of resolution. Mr. North had known it was resolution because, just before that, the other face had confronted this face — each occupying a portion of the screen — and a public address system had said, heavily, "If that's the way you want it." The public address system had answered, instantly, but in a lighter voice, "That's the way it's got to be."

The face faded slowly away, revealing that it was attached to a body. The body had hands, which were held up, in an attitude of rejection. Mr. North knew the attitude was one of rejection because —

163

This was, undoubtedly, the deadliest motion picture he had ever seen. He plodded through his memory. That one three weeks back? The one with a spy in it? (One could tell he was a spy, because he kept pulling down the brim of his hat, even when it was already so far down that he had to bend over backward to see out.) No, this was worse than the spy one. In the spy one there was shooting, toward the end. It had awakened Mr. North. But this was a tale of primitive emotion. A sign outside said so.

Mr. North looked away from the screen and at his wife. She was regarding the picture with fixed attention. Loving it, Mr. North thought bitterly. The things people like! Even Pam. She can sit there, while I'm here dying of boredom, and like this preposterous —

Pam turned just enough so that Jerry could glimpse her companionable smile. She kept her eyes on the screen. Jerry turned his eyes back to it. Loving it, Pam thought bitterly. Of all the incredible bilge! And in addition to everything else, the dress is as wrong for her as it could possibly be. The things I go through to keep that man happy! Sitting here, in the dark, hearing this braying of clichés when I might as well be home finishing the crossword. The master of the *Golden Hind*. Something in five letters ending in — for heaven's sake! *Drake*, of course. With that I could get a whole section. And instead —

"Oh, darling," the loud speaker said, in its more dulcet tones. "Come back, darling — just come back. That's all that's — "

Pam looked away, since the woman on the screen — name of Monica as she recalled it; word in six letters, ending in anguish — was in closeup again, and that was really too much. Jerry was staring at the screen, hanging on every word. Was that, really, the kind of woman he liked? She looked beyond him. Dorian was as intent as Jerry. What on earth was the matter with the two of them? It couldn't be that they really —

About five minutes more of this, Dorian Weigand thought, and I'll scream. That's what I'll do. I'll stand up and scream. Wife of detective captain becomes hysterical in movie, creates disturbance, is ejected. That will serve him right. It will serve everybody right. Pam and Jerry sitting there simply glued to the screen — glued in syrup. When they might be anywhere else; might be talking. It was fun to talk to the Norths, or she had always thought so. Obviously, however, if they were the sort who could be stuck in this — this *treacle* — she must have been wrong in thinking —

I suppose, Jerry thought, I can't spoil their enjoyment. I'll just sit here and — But perhaps if I fidget a little? Not really a great deal. Just toss and turn, slightly? Moan, perhaps? They're nice girls and if they knew what this is doing —

Like a schoolboy, Pam thought. Precisely like a schoolboy. Looks at that overblown so-and-so and simply can't sit still. If I had any gumption I'd just get up and get out of — But I can't do that, because both of them are having such a wonderful —

They're my hosts, Dorian thought. That's one way of looking at it. I'm a poor thing abandoned on Sunday afternoon and they're doing what they can to keep me amused. *Amused!* And I've got to be a little lady and sit and sit and sit and — It changed into something else; into a girl singing on the radio. "I've got to cook and cook and cook — " A catchy tune. She found she was humming it, softly.

"Got to cook and cook and cook," Jerry said, in a whisper. "Love to cook and cook and — "

"Jerry," Dorian said. "I thought you were miles away. Deep in a drama of primitive emotions."

"God," Jerry North said, simply.

They both looked at Pam. And Pamela North said, not entirely in a whisper, "I've had all I can take. Absolutely all. If you two want — "

166

The Norths and Dorian Weigand rose as one, having suffered as three. They went out into the noisy warmth of Eighth Street and stood in the doorway of the theater and looked at Eighth Street. They looked at a delicatessen, two grocery stores and a lunchroom.

"Isn't it beautiful?" Pam said. "Isn't it simply beautiful?"

Jerry waved down a cab.

"Come," Jerry said. "I can still hear it."

Dorian said that she should really go home. But they went to the Algonquin, although it was only a little after six, and too early for dinner. They found Acting Captain William Weigand there, having drinks in the lobby with a very pretty blonde.

It was Dorian who saw Bill first. They had found seats in a corner — the corner nearest the entrance to the Oak Room. Bill and the blonde were in the corner most distant; to see them, Dorian had to look entirely across the pleasant lobby, which is also a cocktail lounge. She had to look past people talking about plays, and people reading *Variety* and people merely waiting for other people. She achieved this.

"Do you," she said, in an especially steady voice, "see what I see? Over there?" She indicated with a movement of her head. The Norths looked. Pam North said, "Oh," in the most indeterminate of tones.

"Speaking," Dorian Weigand said, in the same precisely level voice, "of primitive emotions."

Bill Weigand and the blonde were side by side on a sofa, which was the right size for two. They were turned slightly toward each other, and the blonde was talking. She talked with animation, with smiles. There was a cocktail on a small table in front of her, and Bill held a cocktail in his hand. He listened, and as he listened, he nodded.

"Is that," Dorian said, "supposed to be this cousin? That?"

"Well — " Jerry said.

"There's no use pretending," Pam said. "No. I've seen her somewhere — "

"A Miss Barnscott," Jerry said. "An — er — an actress. In the play, that is."

"Thank you," Dorian said. "You do make things so clear. She's blond, isn't she?"

"Very," Pam said. "Probably a suspect."

"For a suspect," Dorian said, "she's very pretty, isn't she? In a flashy sort of way? A suspect to get drunk with."

"Listen," Jerry said, "you know Bill doesn't get drunk. Or — or anything."

"Doesn't he?" Dorian said. "That's decent of him, isn't it? Goes off to see a cousin. Turns up with — that — that *floozy*."

"As a matter of fact — " Jerry began.

"That's right," Dorian said. "Defend her. Dyes her hair, have you noticed?"

"Look," Jerry said, and there was anxiety in his tone. "You *know* she's a suspect. Or — somebody Bill had to ask something of."

"Don't I," Dorian said. "What I wonder is — ask what of?"

They both looked at her. Then she smiled.

"All right," she said. "She's a suspect. A pretty blond suspect. I trust Bill implicitly. All I don't see is, why can't he have Mullins or somebody talk to the blond ones? All I — "

She broke off. The two across the lobby were rising from the snug sofa. It appeared that Bill was assisting the blonde to arise. It appeared that, having so assisted her, he patted her on one pretty shoulder. It appeared —

"Maybe," Dorian said, "I wasn't kidding anybody. Maybe — "

The blonde — the slim and graceful Miss Phyllis Barnscott — smiled up at Bill Weigand. She held out a hand, which Bill took.

"He," Dorian said, "is squeezing it."

Miss Barnscott's hand was gradually released. She smiled up at Bill again; she flipped the freed hand in a parting gesture. She walked around the end of a head-high partition between lounge and hotel desk, and so toward the door. Bill stood gazing after her.

"If he — " Dorian began, and then Bill turned. He was smiling broadly.

"Swallowed the canary," Dorian said. "If — *oh!*"

It was evident now that Bill Weigand, threading an expert way among chairs and little tables, was headed toward his wife and Pam and Jerry. It was evident that the smile — which had become a grin — was directed toward them. It appeared that Bill Weigand, for a policeman in the middle of a murder investigation, was enjoying himself very much indeed. He stood in front of them, and looked down at them.

*"You!"* Dorian said. "All the time, *you knew we were here!"*

"It is," Bill told her, "the duty of a policeman to be constantly observant."

"You patted her," Dorian said. "If I were a different kind of wife."

"You," Bill said, "would be somebody else's. May I sit down?"

He sat beside Dorian. He patted her shoulder. Jerry North patted the button of a small bell affixed to the table in front of them. A waiter came. Drinks came and they waited.

Phyllis Barnscott, Bill told them, was in a sense an outgrowth of Mrs. Alicia Nelson. He paused while Pam said that that seemed a little — something. He told them of his interview with Mrs. Nelson. He said that she had, he thought, wanted information from him, which was a common desire of people in any degree involved. She had also wanted to give him information about Miss Barnscott. She had not wanted him to meet her husband. At a guess, she had turned her husband loose in a bar, where it seemed entirely probable he would feel at home. He told them that Mr. Nelson wore a stiff straw hat.

"Clean?" Pam asked.

Not, he told her, particularly. And, not a new hat.

"Bleached?" she said.

"Probably," Bill said.

Pam said, "Uh-*huh*" with emphasis.

"The Barnscott — person," Dorian said. "She dyes her hair, you know."

"So she told me," Bill said.

"Open and aboveboard," Dorian said. "The worst type. But — she denied knowing anything. And you believed her."

Bill nodded.

"Otherwise," Dorian said, "you would hardly have — made a spectacle of yourself. Even for our benefit."

"Right," Bill said. "I hardly would have."

"I suppose," Jerry said, "she can prove she didn't kill Fitch?"

That, Bill admitted, was further than he

wanted to go. She had made it seem entirely unlikely. She had been, Bill said, very cheerful about the whole affair, in so far as she was herself concerned. She had said the expected things about the sudden ending of Mr. Fitch. She had said he was a nice boy, and that it was too bad — too damned bad.

"Callous, probably," Dorian said.

Bill smiled at her. She accepted the smile. She patted his hand, in forgiveness, in promise to let it be.

He did not think Phyllis Barnscott was callous. Or, in an accepted sense, hard. He thought she more or less took things as they came.

"Including," Pam said, "Mr. Fitch?"

She had, Bill said, been frank about that — he thought frank. She and Fitch had had "a lot of good times together." She had not specified. But she had said, "I haven't been on a pedestal, captain. Not for years I haven't," leaving him to draw what conclusions he chose and, he thought, not caring greatly what conclusions he did draw. She had said, "He was a nice boy. We went places, and did things. Hurting nobody."

Long before Fitch and Naomi Shaw had "got that way about each other" she and Fitch had got over being any way. That was her story; anybody could tell him it was true.

"There was never any secret about it," she said. "No reason why there should have been. It was a fun game." Nay was a friend of hers. If she wanted Fitch — fine. It was, she assumed, an entirely different thing with Nay and Fitch. Not a "fun thing"; a marriage thing. The idea that she was jealous was preposterous. That, moved by jealousy, she would do anything to hurt anybody —

"You get funny ideas in your business, captain," she said. "It must do things to your mind."

Bill had not told her the source of the theory. He had asked her if she knew the Nelsons.

"The poor old guy ought to join the AA's," she had said. "That's all I know. Oh yes — he used to borrow money from Brad. Had a lot himself when he married Brad's cousin but it went phfft. Mrs. Nelson is interested in clubs and things like that. Wanted to get poor Sammy to talk at one of them."

She had heard of a girl named Peggy Latham; but only, she said, as a girl Brad had once gone around with — oh, yes, and as the kind of girl who rode horses. From what she had heard — although "not from Brad. He wasn't that kind" — she had assumed it was something he was well out of.

"Anyway," she said, and then she had

173

seemed more serious than at any other time, "the way I see it, the way things are nowadays, it's every girl for herself. Don't hurt anybody if you can help it, don't get hurt if you can help it."

"She doesn't," Pam said, "sound like the brooding type."

"Right," Bill said. "That's pretty much what I mean. Also — "

Also, Phyllis Barnscott had told him, she had another iron in the fire. A man he might have heard of wanted her to marry him. For all she knew, she might. A man named Tootle — Jasper Tootle.

"You can laugh," she had said. "He's got a funny name. But he's a nice guy, and we get along fine."

"I'll be damned," Jerry said. "Jasper on a toot."

They listened to that in shocked silence. Jerry North proved himself man enough to apologize.

Bill looked at his watch, then. He said it was early — but. They moved into the Oak Room, and to a table. Over vichyssoise (with just a touch of curry powder) Bill invited an account of their cocktail hour with Samuel Wyatt. They looked at him, and Pam nodded.

"As Mullins says," Bill told them, "I'm clairient."

"I like that," Pam said. "It ought to exist. Also, he's being followed, isn't he?"

He had been, Bill said. He would be again. So far as Bill knew, Wyatt was not being at the moment, having proved elusive, having vanished in Grand Central, which is adapted to disappearances.

"He thinks," Pam said, "that you put in a thumb and pull out a plum. Him. Just like that. Because he found poor Mr. Fitch, chiefly. And because now his royalties don't stop. And because he had a premature allergy." She paused. "Added up," she said, "maybe he's right to be scared."

They waited for Bill.

"And," Bill said, "he wanted to know how he stood? Picking your brains."

"Partly," Jerry said.

"And," Dorian said, "spreading the seeds of suspicion where they might take root. Mrs. Nelson. Mr. Carr. Even Mr. Strothers. He plays the field."

"Right," Bill said. "I'm glad to hear it." He lighted a cigarette between courses and his wife regarded him. He was getting keyed up. He always did. "Movement helps," he said.

"He has got a right to be frightened?" Jerry asked, but was answered only by a shrug. A waiter brought food. At a little after eight they had finished, except for coffee. But then, Bill

Weigand looked again at his watch, and then at Dorian.

"We don't go home, then?" she said, in a tone of resignation.

She did, if she liked. He went back to work. Or, if she preferred —

"Home," she said. "You can at least drop me?"

He could. They left the Norths, who sipped coffee and looked at people, of whom there were not many, since it was a Sunday evening in the month of June. Jerry emptied his cup and said, "Well?"

"If you just sit here long enough," Pam said, "everybody goes by." She nodded her head slightly, and Jerry looked in the direction of the nod. A tall, slightly stooped man — a dark man with dark eyes deeply recessed under jutting brows — was just subsiding into place behind one of the tables for two which Raul of the Algonquin reserves for appropriate guests. Naomi Shaw was already behind the table. She was hatless and in a dark dress. With Wesley Strothers seated beside her, the table was pushed toward them affectionately. Almost simultaneously, drinks arrived.

"Of course," Pam said, "life has to go on. One has to eat."

"Yes," Jerry said. "And — speaking of that. I've still got Braithwaite. If you're — ?"

Pam was. Jerry delayed matters somewhat, multiplying in quest of a percentage. He wrote the figure in, and looked at it doubtfully. Why he always found it so difficult to figure tips he would, he supposed, never know. He shuddered slightly, and pushed the signed check away from him.

"Maybe," Pam said, "you can call it entertainment." She stood up and led the way, so that they passed in front of Miss Naomi Shaw, radiant — but not at the moment appreciably radiant — star of *Around the Corner* and of Mr. Wesley Strothers, its producer. Pam smiled at them, and nodded, but did both with detachment. Naomi Shaw smiled in return, equally without certainty, but by then Jerry had overtaken Pam.

"Evening, Mrs. West," Strothers said. "Hello, West."

They did not argue, but went on. At the door, however, Pam turned and looked back at the two. It appeared that Strothers was doing most of the talking. Naomi Shaw was, apparently, a girl men talked to when they took her out.

"Mr. Strothers has compass trouble," Jerry said, and took Pam by the elbow and through the lobby and into Forty-fourth Street. "Yes, if you will," the last was to the doorman, who offered a cab. But Pam said, "Wait, Jerry.

*Look!*" Jerry looked, as Pam was looking, up Forty-fourth toward Fifth. "The man snapping his fingers," Pam said. "Who else could it be?"

The man, who was narrow, upon whom, seen even from a distance, clothes seemed to hang limply, was passing the Harvard Club. As he walked, he snapped his fingers. As they watched, he stopped, and went to the curb, and looked toward them down Forty-fourth Street, in an unmistakable attitude of a man in search of a cab. He went on again.

"Do you see his tail?" Pam asked.

The doorman looked at her. His mouth opened slowly.

Between them and Samuel Wyatt there was only a couple, but the couple walked toward the Norths. Jerry looked toward Sixth Avenue. Two tall and hatless young men were approaching. Clearly, Jerry thought, en route to the Harvard Club bar.

"No tail," Jerry said.

The doorman blinked his eyes. He left his mouth open.

"Then come on," Pam said, and started on. Jerry overtook her. He said, "Now listen, Pam."

"Slower," Pam said. "We mustn't gain on him. You know that's not the way."

"I know nothing about it," Jerry said, but

slowed his pace to Pam's, to the receding Samuel Wyatt's. "I'm not a tail. I have no ambi-
tion to be — "

"Only until we can get in touch with Bill,"
Pam said. "It's just a — an emergency. We
can't just stand here and let him *go*. You know
that. Only until he holes up. As substitutes."

Jerry ran a hand through his hair. But they
followed Wyatt. Pinch-hitting for tails, Jerry
thought morosely, and hoped that Wyatt soon
would hole.

But he showed no inclination to do this. He
had, it appeared, abandoned his search for
a cab, since he no longer looked back. He
reached Fifth, found the lights with him, and
crossed. The Norths reached Fifth and found
the lights against them. "We can't just stand
here," Pam said, and did not. Jerry caught up
with her in midstream.

"You'll get us both killed," he said, but the
protest was formal.

Wyatt, snapping his fingers at intervals, continued on toward Madison. There the lights
were against him, and he stood obediently on
the curb. Pam drew Jerry to a show window
and looked, with apparent fascination, at a display of office supplies. She was, Jerry thought,
a little overdoing it. "All right," he said, "he's
crossing Madison." They went after him. The
lights changed when they were in the middle

of the avenue and a bus snarled at them. Jerry looked at it haughtily.

"He's going back to Grand Central," Pam said. "It's very suspicious, Jerry. I'm terribly afraid that — "

But at Vanderbilt Avenue, Wyatt turned north. They went after him, cautious around the corner of the building. Wyatt was receding, moving more briskly.

"It's perfectly ridiculous," Pam said, "to be doing this in high heels. If I'd only worn sneakers!"

"You'd have looked odd at the Algonquin," Jerry said. "Anyway, we don't have — "

"He's going toward Park," Pam said. "Let's hurry, Jerry."

They hurried. They reached the end of Vanderbilt Avenue and turned east in Forty-seventh Street. Wyatt was at the corner of Park Avenue. Again he turned north. "I'll bet I know," Pam said.

They followed up Park for several blocks. Wyatt reached a large apartment building. He turned into it. "I knew I knew," Pam said.

They reached the building on the ninth floor of which Bradley Fitch had died. They stopped in front of it.

"Well," Jerry said. "Now what, darling?"

"Now," Pam said, "you find a telephone and tell Bill where he is. I — I'll just lurk."

Bill Weigand sat at his desk in his temporary office in the station house which was the headquarters of Homicide East. Mullins sat in a wooden chair, which was tilted back against the wall. Bill drummed lightly with his fingers on the desk top and Mullins sipped from a cardboard container partially full of a pale liquid which, before milk had been generously added, had been called coffee. Acting Captain Weigand had read for half an hour; he now sought to digest what he had read.

A man had been in Rye. A man had been at a country club in upper Westchester. A man had conferred with the New York State Police at Hawthorne. A man had found, at the Yale Club, an acquaintance whose habitat was Wall Street. A man had reached, by telephone, the executive vice president of a real estate management corporation. Mullins had been, for several hours, in conversation with several men in Chicago. A man had awakened an editor of *Variety* in a hotel bedroom in West Forty-sixth Street. A man had spent the afternoon reading newspaper clippings in the morgue of *The New York Times*. A police department is a creature of many tentacles.

Detective Matthew Rider had waited, on a partially shaded bench, while a man named Omar Patterson (of Patterson, Framingham

& Cohen) had finished a set of tennis with a youth named Bert Collins. Mr. Patterson had won — 6-3 — and had left the court refreshed and in a tolerant mood. Mr. Patterson was sixty-seven; his destroyed antagonist was twenty-two; the sun shone on Mr. Patterson's world, and brightened even the extraneous — Detective (First Grade) Matthew Rider. Matters were, thereby, expedited.

Bill Weigand digested. Bradley Fitch's residuary estate — estimated by Mr. Patterson in the word "phew!" — went to "this pretty actress he was going to marry" — Naomi Shaw, born Mary Shaftlich. To her, also, went the apartment in which Fitch had died. "Barn of a place. Co-op, you know." To her went various articles of jewelry which had been Fitch's mother's. To her, further, went the Southampton estate.

Mrs. Alicia Nelson — "cousin of his, you know" — received a bequest of $25,000. Several other, more distant, relatives received less. "Can't keep it all in my head, you know," Mr. Patterson said, running a towel over the thick gray hair of the head in question. There were relatively small bequests to several servants — one Henry Jones — "or is it Smith?" — got ten thousand; Rose Hemmins got the same amount, and occupancy for life of a cottage on the Long Island estate. Peggy Latham —

"nice girl; more his kind, really" — received Fitch's string of polo ponies.

The will had, since Detective Rider asked, been made quite recently — six weeks ago, two months ago. He'd have to have a look at the instrument itself. The instrument was locked up in his office safe, and if the detective would drop around? The will which was the latest — "the latest we know about, anyway," Patterson said — had superseded a will in which Mrs. Nelson got half the residue, the remaining half being divided among four other relatives. In that previous will, also, there had been a specific bequest of twenty-five thousand to "this other girl of his. Another actress." Rider suggested a name.

"That's right," Mr. Patterson said. "Girl named Barnscott. Went around with her for a while. She gets nothing this time."

Certain personal effects — "watch, that sort of thing" — went to a man named Strothers. "In this will, not the old one."

That was about the size of it, as memory served. Mr. Patterson had returned to the court, this time for doubles; Detective Rider, who was in his early thirties, and a canasta player, had shaken his head admiringly, and sought out a telephone.

James Nelson, who was in his middle sixties, was a retired investment counsellor. "For retired, you can read broke, or damn near it," a man named Foster told his companion over drinks at the Yale Club. His companion, a detective third grade (and also a member of the Yale Club) ordered another round and made encouraging sounds.

"Followed his own advice, is what it came to," Foster said. "One of these guys who inherits something and doesn't know what to do with it. Know the type?" Detective Willings, whose father had undergone the same period of confusion, nodded.

Mr. Nelson had managed to lose his money when all about him were doing nicely, which argued a special sort of talent. Since then he and his wife had been living pretty much on her money. "Some relation to this guy Fitch who got — but you know about that, Freddy."

Freddy Willings nodded. He knew about that.

"Lot younger than he is," Foster said. "Or so I hear. They've got a place up around Rye somewhere. His father's place — probably one of these big barns you can't do anything with. Know the kind I mean?"

Detective Freddy Willings, who owned one, admitted knowing what Foster meant.

"Princeton man," Foster said. "Not that that means anything. Lots of all right guys went to Princeton. Know what I mean?"

"Yes," Freddy Willings said.

"Only thing is," Foster said, "I hear that Nelson's been drinking a lot lately. Sits in a customers' room somewhere — not our shop — and goes out and has a quick one. Has a lot of quick ones. Doesn't keep his wits about him. Know what I mean?"

"Yes."

"What we need," Foster said, "is another drink."

In time, Freddy Willings went to Homicide East and used a typewriter.

Wesley Strothers had been around for some years. Started as a stage manager. "I'm damned if I know how stage managers do start," an editor told a detective. Strothers had done some directing; he had got hold of a script he liked and become a producer. "Only trouble was, he picked a turkey." He had kept at it. He had had other turkeys. He had had a moderate success; then another turkey which had, however, sold well to the movies.

"Money of his own?"

Not that the editor had ever heard of. Got production money from backers. "Like most everybody."

"However, he ought to make plenty now. Since they're not going to close *Corner*. That one's a mine. Hell, it's a uranium mine."

"It's going to keep running, then?"

"That's the word I hear. Damn shame if it doesn't, because it hasn't paid the nut yet and, like I said, it's a mine."

The square man from Kansas City and Chicago, and from Pakistan, Robert Carr, had not, after all, been able to prove that he had been in Chicago when Bradley Fitch was killed. Sergeant Mullins had given him the opportunity, and afterward done what he could to check. A Robert Carr had, certainly, booked a seat on a late plane from LaGuardia on Friday night. He had checked in for the flight. It was, therefore, to be presumed he had made the flight. But it was not, therefore, proved he had made the flight. A Robert Carr had reserved a seat on a return plane, getting in late Saturday. Possibly they would, in time, if necessary, find someone who could testify that Carr had been on the plane. So far, they had not. "Which," Mullins had said in his oral report, "we'll have to admit don't need to mean anything."

Somewhat more interestingly, some hours on the telephone had not enabled Mullins to find anyone in Chicago who could say Carr had been there Saturday. But this, again, did not necessarily mean anything. Asked to be specific, Carr had said that, from the airport, he had gone to his apartment — a small apartment he leased more or less permanently, and

186

sublet when he was in the field. He had made several calls from there, seeking companionship, but had completed none of them. "Nobody stays in Chicago over weekends; not if they can help it."

Giving it up a little after noon Saturday, Carr had, he said, had a lonely drink or two, planning to go out afterward to a solitary lunch. About one o'clock he had turned on the radio and heard a brief report of Fitch's death. "Time fits," Mullins said. "They got out a bulletin fast. And there's the difference in time."

Carr had been sure, talking to Mullins, that the superintendent of the building had seen him when, after hearing the news, he had left and got a cab for the airport. The superintendent, reached — with no little difficulty — by telephone had said, "Sure," and then, "Sure, I guess so," and, finally, "If Mr. Carr says he saw me I must have seen him. Stands to reason, don't it? Course, I see lots of people lots of times." And this was worth nothing.

And Mullins, talking to Robert Carr, had said, all innocence, "Where did you say you were Friday night, Mr. Carr? Before you caught this airplane for Chicago?"

"Why?" Carr asked.

"Just wondered," Mullins said, the innocence persisting. "Told the captain you were

187

tied up, and he assumed it was some business deal. Just like to get things straight."

"What's the point?" Carr said, and Mullins, quite ingenuous, had said he had been told to ask. He had said, as man to man, that it was funny the things the captain wanted to know.

"Consider I'm laughing," Carr said. He paused; seemed to think about it; looked for a long moment, with speculation, at Sergeant Mullins.

"Seems you people get around," he said, then. "O.K. I had a drink with my former wife. Had dinner with her afterward. Had things I wanted to talk to her about."

Mullins waited.

"No," Carr had said then. "I look at you and I say, does he look like Dorothy Dix? and I say, nope, can't say he does."

"All he would say," Mullins had reported. "Can't say I got it."

"He more or less told you," Bill said. "Advice to the lovelorn, sergeant. You write in and say, 'I am only sixteen and my boy friend says all the other girls let their boy friends kiss them good night at least but — '"

"Listen, Loot," Mullins said.

"In other words," Bill said, "Carr was trying to talk her out of marrying Fitch. Or — so he implies."

188

"You think that was it?"

"He may," Bill said, "have been giving her a box of oxalic acid."

Drumming his fingers now, Bill thought of that, and decided that it was one of the possibilities which could not be dismissed. Not perhaps as he had phrased it. But the girl's motive was obvious — it was almost obtrusive. Carr, if he thought to share the money she would inherit, shared her motive. There was no other motive stronger; none he could think of so strong. It would be convenient if that fact answered the question. It had never been his experience that things were necessarily so simple.

There were too many with motives. Naomi's (and Carr's by association) was the strongest. He tried to think of the weakest. Jasper Tootle, in retroactive jealousy, by way of killing Phyllis Barnscott's past? He smiled faintly at the thought. But it was no more ridiculous than situations which had led to murder. People killed, sometimes, for very little — not, say, for a large inheritance, but for a small one which loomed large. Like, he thought, ten thousand dollars in cash and the occupancy of —

The telephone rang.

189

# IX

*Sunday, 8:35* P.M. *to 10:05* P.M.

It is difficult to lurk satisfactorily on Park Avenue; it is particularly difficult on a Sunday evening in June. Lurking is best done where there is cover; one lurks among; a solitary lurker is at a disadvantage. The Park Avenue sidewalks, never so occupied as those of Fifth, so nervously alive as those of Madison, take on an almost embarrassing tranquility on Sunday evenings in summer. Lurking to the best of her ability, Pamela North felt uncomfortably conspicuous.

There were, to be sure, some people about her. Most of them seemed to be walking dogs. With a dog, Pam thought, sauntering distractedly north to the nearest intersection (but snatching watchful peeps over her shoulder toward the entrance of the apartment house) it would be much simpler. A person with a dog lurks of necessity, making frequent halts in a generally aimless progression. The dog explains everything. A cat, even if Pam had happened to have one with her, would have been of no use whatever. There are advantages to dogs, she admitted, grudgingly, and turned and walked down Park again. Dozens of people, at least, were, she was certain, watching her from windows. There had never been a more public lurk.

She passed — and this was for the fourth time, or perhaps the fifth — the entrance to the elderly and dignified apartment house in which Bradley Fitch had died, and into which Samuel Wyatt recently had popped. It was no longer *very* recently, Pam thought, and looked at the watch on her wrist. It was a good quarter of an hour since Jerry had gone off to find a telephone. It was taking Jerry long enough.

The doorman of the apartment house looked at her, Pam decided, very intently. He must think she was out of her mind, or worse. Probably he thought she was casing the place; perhaps at any moment he would call the police and have her arrested for loitering. Loitering with intent. Or was that something you could do only in Britain? If only she had a dog. Even a small dog. Even a Peke. Temporarily, of course, because what the cats would do to a Peke hardly bore thinking about. What they would do to a Great Dane, for that matter.

Having passed the entrance, Pam was now constrained to resume looking over her shoulder from time to time to make sure Wyatt did not pop out again unobserved. This, Pam thought, is going to give me a crick in the neck. Wherever did Jerry *go?* Surely it shouldn't take him all this time to find a telephone here in the middle of the city of New York. Of course, there isn't much open on Park this time of a Sunday. Even on Madison — perhaps he's had to go clear down to Grand Central.

She reached the cross street below the apartment house. She stopped on the curb. She snapped her fingers — that was it. She snapped them again for good measure, becoming a person who had suddenly thought of something. A woman, say, who had just at that moment remembered she had left something turned on at home and had to hurry back to turn it off. Pam North walked briskly north, her heels clicking on the pavement, a look of intentness on her face. People probably would think she had absent-mindedly left the baby in the bath.

The up-and-down-town blocks in Manhattan are short blocks. It takes hardly any time to walk one. (Particularly when you are hurrying before the baby drowns.) Almost at once, Pam found herself at the next intersection. Now what? She hesitated at the curb, as if to let traffic pass. Unfortunately, there was no traffic. If she turned into the cross street, toward Madison, she would be out of sight of the apartment house. Wyatt might come out and go away, un-tailed. Of course, she could just stand there. Stand there and — say — look at her watch indignantly from time to time, so becoming a woman waiting with lapsing patience, to be met.

She did look at her watch. It had now been a good twenty minutes. *Good* twenty minutes indeed! One of the most annoying twenty minutes she could remember. Of course, there had been the time she had been locked in a closet somewhere in Westchester. And the time she had been in a glass case with a prehistoric man. But those times had not been, in the proper sense, annoying. Was it conceivable that Jerry had gone all the way back to the apartment to telephone? Was it even remotely —

She looked down the side street, toward Madison, and there was Jerry. He was hurrying; it was hardly too much to say he was loping. At least he knew he had taken an inexcusable time to telephone Bill Weigand. Leaving her holding the bag, conducting an uncompanioned lurk. He'd better have a good ex —

Abruptly, the air was filled with the wailing of sirens. A patrol car came through the side street, flashed past Jerry North — who checked his lope and stared at it — and at Park turned south. There was another patrol car coming down Park. And another coming *up* Park. And another —

Jerry resumed his lope, and joined Pam at the corner. Together they looked down the avenue, watched four patrol cars of the New York City Police Department lurch to a stop in front of the apartment house and stand there, panting, while policemen spurted from them. And they heard, coming up Park, a siren with a slightly different tone. A squad car, screaming about it, U-turned from the north-bound roadway (going the wrong way at the cross-over) and a taxicab stopped, as if on hind legs, to let it pass — to let it nose in at the apartment house.

"Well," Pam said, "you certainly hit the jackpot, didn't you?"

"What?" Jerry North said. "Oh. I didn't even get Bill. A detective somebody. Said Bill had just — "

Another siren interrupted him. A convertible Buick was streaking north, and from it the siren's wail was coming. The Buick turned as the squad car had turned.

" — had just gone out," Jerry said.

"Just come in," Pam said. "Come on!" She began to run toward the clustering police cars. "Something must have happened," she said, panting a little. "Unless — " she checked her pace. *"Jerry!"* she said. "The doorman — he looked at me so suspiciously. Do you suppose he decided that — *oh!"* She stopped. She began to move forward, but more slowly. "I'll have to give myself up," she said. "What will they — "

But she did not finish. Bill and Sergeant Mullins emerged from either side of Bill's convertible. They did not exactly run, but they did not exactly walk.

"Bill," Pam called. "I was just — "

Her voice reached Bill Weigand. He looked at her for an instant; he nodded and made a quick beckoning gesture. He said something to a policeman at the door. But neither he nor Mullins waited.

The Norths went on. The policeman at the door moved toward them.

"You the Norths?" he said and, without waiting for an answer, "Captain wants you to wait around."

"But," Pam North said. "It's a public street. Public as any street I know. If a person can't walk on Park Avenue without — without all this — where can she walk?"

The policeman looked at her. His mouth opened slightly.

Mrs. Rose Hemmins had died wearing a

black dress — a respectable black dress. But she had died of a gunshot wound in the chest, and there was a great deal of blood on the dress and on the floor around her. Not all the blood was hers. Some of it had come from the shattered body of a big black cat.

The two bodies lay on the floor of Mrs. Hemmins' sitting room, in the rear of the apartment. The room was surprisingly cold. The air-conditioning unit in the window hummed heavily; it was set to maximum, although the night was only pleasantly warm. Bill Weigand stepped carefully through the room and reached the window and looked out through the pane above the unit. The window opened on a court — not a large court. He went out of the room and into the big kitchen, and to a window in it which also opened on the court. He opened the window. The sound of the whirring unit was very loud in the court. He closed the window and went back into the small sitting room, which was inconveniently full of men doing those things which must be done when there is violent death. An assistant medical examiner sat on his heels by the body, trying to avoid the drying blood. He stood up when Weigand returned.

"Fairly close range," he said. "Probably a .32. Got her through the heart."

"Right," Bill said. "The cat?"

The physician went to look at the cat. He picked the black body up and held it dangling in his hands. The long black hair was matted with the cat's blood.

"Same thing," he said. "Bullet went through. You'll find it around somewhere."

He put the cat's body down on the floor.

"How long did she live afterward?" Bill asked.

"Didn't," the doctor said. "Not what you could call that. Technically, maybe a few seconds."

"She couldn't have moved? Tried to stop the blood?"

"With that?" the assistant medical examiner said, and pointed at the wound.

"Right," Bill said, and watched them begin to take pictures.

"Closeup of the towel, or whatever it is," Bill said, and the photographer looked at him with the expression of a man whose knowledge of his business had been assailed. But he took a closeup of the cloth wadded in Mrs. Hemmins' clenched right hand.

There were only spots of blood on the cloth. The towel had not, evidently, been used in an effort to stanch the flow of blood. If the assistant medical examiner was right, as presumably he was, it could not have been. Unless the cat had been shot first?

"Standing when she was shot?" Weigand asked the physician. The physician shrugged. "At a guess," Bill said.

"At a guess, yes."

"How long ago?"

"At a guess, within an hour. Not much more than that, anyway. An hour and a half, perhaps, from when I got here, of course."

Bill looked at his watch. It showed nine thirty-five. The assistant medical examiner had been there about ten minutes.

"Not before, say, seven-thirty," the doctor said. "Not later than about a quarter of nine. I'm guessing, you know. And it's cold in here."

"Right," Bill said. The doctor closed his bag; wrote in a black notebook. The doctor went.

After a few minutes, Bill also left the little sitting room — the cold little room, which was filled with the humming of an air-conditioning unit, turned high to muffle the sound of shots.

Samuel Wyatt was sitting, on a straight chair although there were more comfortable chairs around him, in the larger of the two big rooms between the suite which had been Rose Hemmins' and the entrance foyer. He sat dolefully. As Bill Weigand came into the room, Wyatt looked up. He was sniffling; he held a handkerchief in his hand and dabbed his nose with it, and dabbed his running eyes. He snapped the fingers of his free hand, and did so disconsolately. A uniformed policeman stood watching him.

"All I did — " Wyatt said.

"In a minute, Mr. Wyatt," Bill told him, and went on into the foyer, and then out of the apartment to the small, furnished room at which the elevator stopped. Pam and Jerry North sat side by side on the small sofa, as if in a doctor's waiting room. They stood up together when Bill came out of the apartment.

"All right," Bill said, "what have you been up to?"

"I was just walking up and down," Pam said. "I had a perfect right to. I — "

"We were following Wyatt," Jerry said. "From the Algonquin — from Forty-fourth Street, anyway — to here. Your men had lost him, remember? We found him for you."

"All I was doing," Pam said, "was waiting to see if he came out again. While Jerry telephoned. It took him hours, but I wasn't *doing* anything. Nothing for everybody to get excited — " She stopped suddenly. "What *has* happened?" she asked. "Not all this to pick up a — a suspicious woman."

"Your friend Wyatt has found another body," Bill told them. "Two bodies, to be exact. The housekeeper's. Her cat's. At least, he says he has."

"The *cat?*" Pam said. "Somebody killed the *cat?* Too? Why would anybody kill the cat?"

"Or," Bill said, "Mrs. Hemmins?"

"People are different," Pam said. "I mean — there are reasons to kill people."

"I don't know, Pam," Bill said. "When did Wyatt get here?"

"About eight-thirty," Jerry said.

Bill Weigand nodded, slowly. He hesitated.

"Wait a few more minutes," he said. "I'll send somebody out for you."

He went back into the apartment.

"I don't," Pam North said, "see why anybody would kill the cat. Unless — " She paused. Jerry waited. "No," she said, "it might seem like that, but it wouldn't be. Or, I shouldn't think so. He said he liked them."

She looked at the red door to the apartment, but she did not seem to see it. . . .

"Now," Bill said, "tell me what happened, Mr. Wyatt."

Wyatt looked up at him for a moment. Then Wyatt put his handkerchief in his pocket and snapped the fingers of his right hand, as if to emphasize a decision.

"I've got a right not to say anything," he said. "That's the law, isn't it?"

"Right," Bill said. He turned to the patrolman. "Get Sergeant Mullins, will you?" he asked, and the patrolman went. Bill Weigand pulled a chair near and sat down on it. Wyatt set his thin face in an expression of determination. But then he sneezed violently and clutched for his handkerchief, brought it out again. "Damn," he said.

"Must be a nuisance," Bill said. "However, the cat's dead now."

Wyatt started to say something, but instead sneezed again. Mullins came from the direction of the small cold room in the rear of the apartment. The uniformed man came after him. Bill Weigand stood up.

"Oh, sergeant," Bill said. "Mr. Wyatt doesn't want to make a statement. Quite within his rights, of course. So, take him over to the precinct, will you? See he has a chance to call a lawyer. Then, book him on suspicion of homicide."

"O.K., Loot," Mullins said. "Come on, mister."

"So that's the way it is," Wyatt said. "Just like that. No need to look any further, huh? Make it easy for yourselves."

"Talk to your lawyer, Mr. Wyatt," Bill said. "Best thing you can do, probably. Since you have things to hide."

"Got me coming and going, haven't you?"

Wyatt said. He made no move to get up from the chair. He sneezed again. "Damn cats," he said. "All right, what do you want to know?"

"Whatever you can tell us," Bill said. "You do want to talk? The sergeant will take down what you say. It will be put in statement form and you'll be asked to sign. And —"

"Used in evidence," Wyatt said. "Hell, I've written this scene, captain."

"We're wasting time," Bill said. "How did you happen to be here?"

"Rang the bell," Wyatt said. "Nobody answered so I got hold of the superintendent and got him to unlock the door and —"

"Right," Bill said. "We've talked to the superintendent. You know what I mean. How did you happen to be here at all? You wanted to see Mrs. Hemmins?"

"Yes. I was walking along and came by here and decided to stop in and talk to her."

"Why? What about?"

Wyatt sneezed again. The sneeze, to Weigand, did not seem entirely spontaneous. Wyatt put the handkerchief he had been using back in a pocket of his trousers. He took a fresh handkerchief from the breast pocket of his jacket. He wiped his eyes.

"O.K.," he said, finally. "I don't like the spot I'm in. So, I'm not just sitting around and doing nothing. I figured Mrs. Hemmins might know something that would help. Anyway — help me to know where I stood."

"Investigation on your own?"

"You can call it that."

"Or — you wanted to try to get her to change her story? Say that you didn't show signs of this allergy of yours before you came into the apartment Saturday?"

"There it is again," Wyatt said. "Coming and going." He snapped his fingers, this time wearily. "What's the use?"

"Was that it?"

"No, that wasn't it. Just wanted to see — well, maybe she noticed something I didn't, when we found Fitch. Maybe — how do I know? She might know something that would be a help. Just fishing, if you want to know."

"You were just walking by. Thought, 'I'll go talk to Mrs. Hemmins.' Came up here and when she didn't answer, instead of just assuming she'd gone to a movie, got hold of the superintendent and got him to let you in?"

"Believe it or not," Wyatt said.

"Where had you been before you walked by here?"

"Having dinner. At the Commodore Bar."

Bill Weigand shook his head.

"If I were you," he said, "I *would* talk to a lawyer. Better take him along, sergeant."

Mullins said, "O.K. Come on, mister."

203

"Tell your lawyer Mrs. Hemmins' story put you in the apartment Saturday earlier than you admitted you had been in it. Put you upstairs about the time Fitch died. And he'll tell you that, if Mrs. Hemmins didn't make a formal statement — and perhaps even if she did — what she said won't hurt anybody in legal proceedings, because now she's dead."

"So that's it?" Wyatt said. "All worked out."

"You weren't just passing here," Bill said. "You didn't come here from the Commodore. Nobody gets a superintendent to open an apartment house door merely because the bell isn't answered. You'd better get a lawyer."

Wyatt looked at him. He looked at him for some seconds.

"Ask the Norths to come in, will you, sergeant?" Bill said. "They're in the outside hall." Mullins went. He returned with the Norths, and Wyatt had said nothing, although he had sneezed again.

"Mr. Wyatt says he came here from the Commodore," Bill told Pam and Jerry North.

"Why, Sam!" Pam said. Jerry shook his head, a little sadly.

"They saw you," Bill told Wyatt. "Near the Algonquin. In Forty-fourth Street. They knew I'd had you followed and that my man had lost you. So — they followed you instead."

"My friends," Wyatt said. "My ever loyal friends. My publisher."

"Followed you here," Bill said. "Watched you go in. Tried to notify me. But — by that time the superintendent had called and told us about Mrs. Hemmins, and we were on the way here."

"I told him to do that," Wyatt said. "He'll tell you I did."

"Right," Bill said. "He has told me. He's also said that you were very insistent about getting in. Said something must have happened to Mrs. Hemmins." He paused. "Want to have another try at it, Mr. Wyatt?"

Wyatt looked long at Bill Weigand. He looked at the Norths. He told them, with a little bitterness, that they had been a big help. He said, "All right, I left one or two things out." He mopped his still running eyes and, in an aside, again damned all cats. He had another try at it.

It was true, Wyatt said — and now he began to talk rapidly, a little jerkily — that he had had dinner at the Commodore Bar. It was true that, after dinner, although he had been too nervous to eat much —

"Why?" Bill asked him.

"My God, man," Wyatt said. "Who wouldn't be? You think I don't know how it looks to you people?"

"Go ahead," Bill said.

After dinner, Wyatt had walked up Park Avenue. Worrying. "Kept writing a scene about being in the death cell. One I told the Norths about." He had been about half a block from the apartment house when he had seen "this fellow" go into it.

"Who?"

"O.K. Wes. Wes Strothers."

Strothers had gone in as if he were in a hurry. Wyatt had thought it was "funny."

"Why?"

"His friend Fitch is dead. Who would he be hurrying to see?" Wyatt snapped his fingers. "Hell," he said. "I don't know why I thought it was funny. Except — I was looking for something funny. See what I mean?"

"Go on," Bill said.

"That's what I didn't do," Wyatt said. "I waited. Walked up and down and — "

"No wonder the doorman was puzzled," Pam said. "All evening, people lurking." They looked at her. "It doesn't matter," Pam said. "I was just thinking."

Wyatt snapped his fingers and shrugged at the same time, dissociating himself. He had patrolled the block for, he thought, about fifteen minutes. He had been at the upper end of the block when Strothers came out again. Strothers seemed still to be in a hurry. He had stood at the curb and waved at cabs. "Including some anybody could see were taken." He had also looked, several times, up and down the avenue. Wyatt, stepping close to a building — looking around the corner of a building, actually — had watched the tall, slightly stooped, producer of his play.

"Why?"

"I don't know. The way he acted. Fidgety."

A cab had stopped for Strothers after a few minutes. On an impulse, Wyatt had waved down a cab for himself, being lucky. He had had the cab follow Strothers.

This time, Bill did not ask why.

Wyatt had followed the producer to the Algonquin, and followed him into it — or part way into it. He had seen him meet Naomi Shaw and, with her, start toward the entrance of the Oak Room.

"Then I decided to come back here," Wyatt said. "Try to find out what he'd been up to."

"Why did you think he'd been up to anything?"

Wyatt looked hard at Weigand.

"Somebody has," he said. "You think I have. You're willing to settle for me. Think I don't know?"

"So," Bill said, "you're merely trying to be helpful."

"To save my own skin. You want me to go on? Or am I just wasting your time?"

"Go on."

Wyatt had walked back to the apartment house. "With these friends of mine following me." He had gone up to the apartment, and rung the bell several times and, after it remained unanswered, gone to find the superintendent.

"Don't ask me why, except that I thought something had happened. He'd got in."

He didn't know that, Bill pointed out. He did not know Strothers had gone there to see Mrs. Hemmins. He did not know that, if he had gone to see her, he had found her in the apartment.

"A quarter of an hour he was inside," Wyatt said. "It wouldn't take five minutes to find out she didn't answer. It didn't take me five minutes to find out she didn't answer. And — the superintendent hadn't let anybody else in. He told me that when I asked him."

Wyatt had found the superintendent. Together they had found the body of Rose Hemmins — and the body of Toby, her cat. The superintendent had reported what they had found. "And that," Wyatt said, "is all I know about it." He looked at Bill Weigand with resolution; with an expression affirming innocence. Unfortunately, the expression was disrupted by another sneeze. The poor man, Pam North thought. Just when he was registering.

Sam Wyatt stood, then. He held his hands out, side by side, the fists clenched. "All right," he said, "put them on."

Bill let him stand so for a moment. Then Bill said, "No, Mr. Wyatt. The tumbril isn't ready yet. I'll let you know when it is."

Wyatt looked at the acting captain of Homicide East.

"You know," Wyatt said, "I don't think I like you." He snapped his fingers. "I'm damned sure I don't," he said. But then he sneezed again. "Oh, *hell*," Sam Wyatt said. "Let me get out from where there're cats."

"Wherever you like," Bill Weigand told him. "For now."

Wyatt was surprised. He showed it. It occurred to Pamela North that he was, indeed, almost disappointed. You write a scene, she thought, and it doesn't play the way you thought it would. You sneeze, and nobody puts handcuffs on at cue and — I wonder, Pam thought, if he's writing the whole thing? Or — if he wants us to think he is? Writers are such funny people. If, of course, they're all like poor Sammy. Imagining everything out in advance.

As Wyatt went, a thin — a curiously rejected — figure, in search of purer air, Sergeant Mullins lifted enquiring eyebrows. "Right," Bill said, and Mullins went to see to it.

"Well," Jerry North said, flatly. "You think he's the one?"

"I'm not," Bill said, "as sure as he seems to think I am. He tells a circumstantial story. Lots of nice detail. But — " He did not finish, although he was given time.

"Sometimes," Jerry said, "a writer becomes a figment of his own imagination. Sometimes you can see them at it."

"Only," Pam said, "you can't always tell which is which. And sometimes there are — oh, figments within figments." She paused. "If I know what I mean," she added. "Anyway, I think it's very strange about the poor cat."

"I — " Bill began and then said, to a blond young man who had come in from the elevator foyer and stood just inside the door, "Yes, Freddy. You want to see me?"

Detective Frederick Willings — who sometimes thought people would still be calling him Freddy when he was ninety — said, "If you've got a moment, captain," and came over. He looked, with a policeman's doubt of civilians, at the Norths. He was told to go ahead. He went ahead.

Pursuant to instructions, he had been talking to the superintendent of the building, to the doorman, to the operator on duty in the elevator which served the Fitch apartment. The doorman had said that there had been a woman hanging around suspiciously just before the police arrived. "We'll check on that," Bill Weigand told him gravely, pointedly not looking at Pam North.

The superintendent of the building, who had a flat on the ground floor, was shocked by the whole business — personally shocked by what he had seen; shocked in behalf of the owners of the building by this second blow to the building's dignity. He had had a drink or two to steady himself. He found it difficult to tell what things were coming to.

He had not let anyone into the apartment before he let Mr. Wyatt in. Mr. Wyatt had seemed excited and upset when he had come asking to be let in. He had kept snapping his fingers, which proved he was excited and upset. He had been sure something must have happened to Mrs. Hemmins. "Turned out he was right, didn't it?" the superintendent said, and Freddy Willings had agreed that it had. Who else might have visited the apartment previously, if anybody had, the superintendent wouldn't know. Maybe Roy, on the elevator, would. Except maybe he had been eating and put the car on automatic. He was supposed to eat about eight, and not take more than half an hour at it.

Roy, who was elderly, had been eating from about eight until around eight-thirty. He had had no relief, and had left the elevator at the first floor, set for automatic operation. "Most of our people go away weekends," Roy said. "Like you'd expect." There was no way of knowing whether the elevator had been used in his absence. It had been at the first floor when he returned to it.

During the earlier part of the evening? Before he went to eat? And, after he returned?

Just after he returned — this skinny man, up *and* down, ringing like he was in an awful hurry when he wanted to be brought down; asking where he could find the super; finding the super and going up with him. After that — "You people. Cops. Never saw so many cops."

Before?

Before eight — about ten minutes before eight — a couple. The woman "skinny," maybe forty, maybe fifty. The man considerably older, wearing the kind of straw hat you didn't see so often any more. The man had been drinking, but he didn't show it too much. "Smelled like it, though." The couple had got off on the eighth floor and had crossed the foyer to the door of the Fitch apartment. Whether they had got in, he didn't know. He assumed they had, since they had not rung to be brought down before he went to eat. For all he knew, they were still "up there."

His report finished, Freddy Willings, neatly dressed but with a police shield pinned to his coat, as is required of detectives at the scene of a crime, waited.

"The man with the straw hat," Pam North said. "The *bleached* straw hat."

"Apparently," Bill said.

"But," Pam said, "Mrs. Hemmins was shot, wasn't she? And Toby, too? Don't people always use the same methods?"

"No," Bill said. "Freddy, I want you to go to the Barclay. See a Mr. and Mrs. James Nelson."

"Yes sir," Freddy Willings said.

"Ask them," Bill told him, "if they killed Mrs. Hemmins and her cat."

"Right," Willings said. He turned, almost military in his precision, and started for the door. Bill looked at him with a little doubt.

"Freddy," Bill said, and Detective Willings stopped. "Not in precisely those words, perhaps."

"No sir," Freddy Willings said.

"A good detective is always more or less suspicious and very inquisitive," Bill said. "I

213

quote from the Manual of Procedure, Freddy. Find out what the hell the Nelsons were doing here."

"Yes sir," Freddy said, and went to do it. Bill Weigand watched him go, smiling faintly. He turned to Pam North. He said, "You're a housewife, aren't you?"

"What on earth?" Pam said. "Yes. I suppose so. If you like pigeonholes."

"Wait a minute," Bill said, and went and returned. He carried wadded cloth. There were spots of blood on it. He shook it out and it dangled, wrinkled badly, from his hand. It was, now, evidently a tea-towel, banded in red at top and bottom. He asked Pam what she made of it.

"Well," Pam said, "it's a tea-towel." She swallowed. She said she supposed that that was blood on it.

"Oh, yes," Bill said, dismissing the blood. "A wrinkled tea-towel."

They waited.

"Mrs. Hemmins had dressed herself in a black dress," Bill said. "Black silk dress — or rayon or nylon or something of the kind. Dressed herself up, I'd think. Because she knew somebody was coming. And — she had this tea-towel wadded up in her hand. And, she wasn't wearing an apron." He stopped and waited for Pam North, who looked at the cloth and after a bit said, "Well?" Then she held out her hand and took the towel.

"It's dry," she said. She held it up. "It was damp and somebody wadded it up damp and it dried that way. Anybody can see that by looking at it."

"Not a freshly laundered towel she'd picked up and wadded in her hand?"

"That would *look* different," Pam said. "This one was used and then, instead of being shaken out and hung on a rack or something, it was just — well, wadded up." She looked at it more carefully, and shook her head. She held it out to Bill Weigand. She said, "Is there something special about it? Outside of careless housekeeping?"

"I don't know," Bill said. "She wasn't dressed for washing dishes. And, as you say, the towel's dry now. If it had just been used, you'd expect it to be damp."

"It means something?"

"I haven't the faintest idea," Bill Weigand said. "I'm just inquisitive, as I reminded Freddy Willings to be."

# X

*Sunday, 10:20* P.M. *to Monday, 1:05* A.M.

Naomi Shaw had a house of her own. Samuel
Wyatt had a small, but comfortable, suite in
an apartment hotel. Phyllis Barnscott lived at
the Algonquin; the James Nelsons — now
presumably explaining themselves to Detective Freddy Willings, who it was to be hoped
talked Mrs. Nelson's language — had a house
in Rye.

But Mr. Wesley Strothers, who employed
Miss Shaw and Miss Barnscott, who paid royalties to Sam Wyatt, lived in the westward
reaches of Bank Street. Bank Street is a street
in the Village; it is one of those streets which
are hard for cab drivers to discover; it is not an
impressive street. The house in which Wesley
Strothers lived was not an impressive house.
Acting Captain Weigand went up a short flight
of sandstone steps, which were flaking off, and
opened a heavy door and went into a small
vestibule, which was almost completely dark.
Weigand struck a match and examined push-
buttons. Strothers lived on the third floor.

Weigand pressed the button several times, and was unanswered. He went out to the sidewalk and looked up at the windows of the third floor. They were unlighted. Weigand went back to his car and sat in it. The radio talked to itself, speaking, harshly, of trials and tribulations, and of the need of patrol cars to cope therewith.

He sat in the car for almost half an hour, and smoked several cigarettes and — toward the end a little sleepily — sought among the facts he had for the hunch he needed. The hunch remained elusive. Presumably, this meant that he still lacked facts. It was to be hoped that that was what it meant. He named names to himself — Naomi Shaw; her former husband, Robert Carr; Alicia and James Nelson; Phyllis Barnscott; Peggy Latham, who had (perhaps) sought love and had come up with polo ponies. But perhaps they were an adequate substitute; Miss Latham was only a name, brought to his attention. Miss Latham had a brother. Bill had to search memory for his name. Arnold Latham, Jr. So far, a character created by Naomi Shaw. And Samuel Wyatt — to some extent, as Jerry had suggested, a character created by Samuel Wyatt.

Bill had, before, run into such people as these. They had proved not so much puzzling as elusive. You sought to put a finger on them,

217

and they were not there. They were performing versions of themselves; they were writing characters for themselves, and scenes for the characters to play. Wyatt, now — imagining himself arrested, imagining himself in the death cell at Sing Sing, filling in all the details, presumably with dialogue. Living it all out in his mind. James Thurber's Walter Mitty? Or a man staring, hopelessly, into a future shaped by his own actions? "Figments within figments," Pam North had said. Sometimes things Pam said kept going round and round in the mind like — like rolling drops of mercury. "Figments within — "

A cab stopped behind Bill's Buick. Bill watched it in the mirror. A tall man, a little stooped, a bare-headed man with dark hair, got out of the cab and paid, and went up the sandstone steps. The cab pulled out, went on through Bank Street. Bill allowed several minutes. He went back to the dark vestibule, and lighted another match, and pressed the proper button. After a little time, the door in front of him clicked, in apparent excitement. Bill climbed stairs — the house listed to his right, and the stairs were tilted accordingly — to the third floor. Wesley Strothers stood in a doorway with the light behind him. He said, "Yes?" He listened. He said, "Sure. But isn't it pretty late?" He was told there were just a few points.

The apartment comprised two small rooms, with a kitchenette behind a curtain in a corner of one, and a bathroom between. The floors of both rooms canted, in accordance with the weary subsidence of the elderly house. The furniture was worn. Bill, directed, sat in what would, he supposed, be described as a "comfortable old chair." He found it merely old.

"Not much of a place, is it?" Wesley Strothers said. He had a deep, pleasant voice. He was, Bill realized, younger than one thought on seeing him first. The stoop misled, probably. And deep-set eyes somehow suggest advancing years. At a guess — a second guess — Wesley Strothers was not over forty. Perhaps he was a few years under forty. "Lived here for five-six years," Strothers said. "Waiting for a hit. Or for the place to fall down. I'd begun to think it would fall down first, and then Sammy came along with this script of his." He paused. "Well?" he said.

"Probably you'll move now," Bill said.

"First of October," Strothers said. "God, yes."

"Now that the play is going to keep running?"

"You people get around, don't you?" Strothers said. "Look, can't I get you something. Brandy? Or coffee, for that matter?"

Bill shook his head, while saying, "Thanks, no."

He wouldn't mind, he was told, if Strothers made himself coffee. "Drink a lot of coffee." Bill would not. He watched Strothers, who pulled back the curtain of the kitchenette, lighted a two-burner stove, put a percolator over the flame. He wiped out the inside of a cup. "Got most of my meals on this until a few months ago," he said, pointing at the stove. "Eating better, now. But things get dusty. Sure you won't have a cup?"

Bill thanked him again.

Strothers remained by the kitchenette. He looked down at Weigand.

"I'd begun to feel left out," Strothers said. "Get a long statement from Nay. Put Sammy through it. Must have made him snap his fingers a lot. Writers are funny, but I suppose we've got to have them. Or go back to the *commedia dell'arte*." He looked at Bill Weigand with sudden doubt. "Improvisation, you know," he said.

"Yes," Bill said. "It takes time to get around to everyone, Mr. Strothers. You did give us a statement."

"That I was here, eating breakfast, when you say poor Brad was killed," Strothers said. "That I didn't know of any enemies he had."

"Right," Bill said.

220

"Now," Strothers said, "you want me to go over it in detail, I suppose?"

Absently, Wesley Strothers continued to dust out the inside of the coffee cup. Then he put the cup down and hung the tea-towel on a rod. He shook the percolator slightly, as if to arouse it. He opened the door of the small refrigerator which was under the gas plate and bent down and found what he wanted, and came up with a bottle of cream. Bill waited for the completion of these domestic chores.

"Mrs. Hemmins has been killed," he said, then, in a conversational tone.

Wesley Strothers put the cream bottle on a counter. He put it there very carefully. He drew in a deep breath. He said, "God!" He said, "Not *Rosie!*"

"Yes," Bill said. "Rose Hemmins. And her cat. They were both shot."

The tall, dark man left the kitchenette and took the step or two needed to bring him near the middle of the small room. He stood there, looking down at Bill Weigand from caverned eyes.

"When did it happen? Just a few hours ago she — " He stopped. He shook his head slowly, "Why?" he said. "For God's sake, *why?*"

"I suppose," Bill said, "because she knew something. Perhaps tried to cash in on what she knew."

"Rosie?" Strothers said. "It'd be the last — " He did not finish. He gestured bewilderment with both hands. "When did you say it happened?"

"This evening," Bill told him. "We don't know the exact time. Three or four hours ago, probably. Have you seen her recently, Mr. Strothers?"

Strothers looked down at Weigand, his dark eyes intent, and for a moment did not reply. But then, slowly, he began to nod his head. He pulled a chair around to face Weigand and sat down in the chair.

"Yes," he said. "This evening. From what you say, it must have been just before she was killed." He shook his head again. "The poor old thing," he said. "She was all dressed up. As if she were going out some place. A movie, maybe. And now she's dead. Shot, you said? And — the cat, too?"

"Yes," Bill said.

"She was fond of the cat," Strothers told him. "Thought more of the cat than — well, she thought a lot of the cat." He leaned forward, suddenly. "She was dressed up because somebody was coming," he said. "Not because she was going out."

"Probably," Bill said. "How did you happen to be there, Mr. Strothers?"

Wesley Strothers was staring at the floor.

222

For a moment, it appeared that he had not heard. But then he said, "Oh. I went to see whether she'd work for me this fall." He looked up. "Housekeeper, you know," he said. He waved at the apartment. "Going to go the whole hog," he said. "From rags to riches. From two rooms to five. I'll have to get somebody, and I thought of Rosie."

He had, he said, thought of her as a possible keeper of his new apartment that evening. He had "had an engagement uptown anyway," and had left early enough to go by the Park Avenue apartment. He had, he thought, got there around eight. The elevator was unattended and he had ridden up to the eighth floor, rung the doorbell, been admitted by Mrs. Hemmins. He had talked to her briefly. She had agreed to take the job.

"Pleased about it, poor old girl," Strothers said. "Kept on thanking me — saying she hadn't known what she was going to do or where she was going to go. That sort of thing. Thought once she was — hell, going to kiss me."

"You talked to her in her room?" Weigand asked.

Strothers said he had not. They had talked — it hadn't taken long — in the room just beyond the entrance foyer.

"I didn't have too much time," Strothers

said. "I had an engagement."

"With Miss Shaw," Bill said. "Yes."

For a moment Strothers looked puzzled. Then he said, "Oh, that fellow East."

Strothers said he had offered to advance Mrs. Hemmins money to tide her over until she went to work for him, and that she had said that wasn't necessary — yet, anyway. Then Strothers had left.

"When you were with her," Bill said. "She wasn't carrying anything?"

"Carrying anything?"

When her body was found, Bill told him, she had been clutching a wadded up tea-towel.

Strothers shrugged. He said he didn't remember anything like that. Had she been wearing an apron? Strothers was sure she had not. Did the tea-towel mean anything? Because it seemed to him that there would be a dozen ways of explaining it. Perhaps, for example, she had spilled something on her dress, and had got a towel to wipe it off.

"Perhaps," Bill said. "At first, she didn't act to you as if she were expecting anyone?"

Strothers looked at the floor again, his eyes narrowed. Then he shook his head. Then he said, "No, I didn't think that, exactly. Not then. Now it's pretty obvious."

Bill waited. Strothers looked up at him.

"I don't like to say this," he said. "Probably

nothing to it. But — when I was getting a cab after I'd talked to the poor old girl I thought I saw somebody I knew. In front of the building. He was a good way off and I was in a hurry and — you know how it is?" He waited. Bill Weigand waited, too. "Got in the cab and said to myself, 'Wasn't that Sam Wyatt?'"

"And you couldn't be sure?"

"Nope. Didn't matter anyway. Or — didn't then. Chances are it was just somebody who looked like him. Only — well, there it is. For what it's worth. You can ask him."

"It was Mr. Wyatt," Bill told him. "He mentioned seeing you, Mr. Strothers."

"So? That's what brought you here? Well — I'm glad I didn't try to hide I'd seen her. I thought of it, there for a moment. Thought, what's the use? Just get myself involved. Just as well I didn't. I suppose I oughtn't to tell you I even thought of it."

It was a very natural impulse, Bill told him; an impulse very wisely resisted.

"So," Strothers said. "I didn't kill the poor old girl, if that's what you were thinking. Just offered her a job. Left her — smiling. All dressed up and smiling, and with the cat rubbing against her legs, the way they do." He paused. "You think she knew something? About Brad's death?"

It was, Bill told him, the most likely possibility, and at that Strothers nodded, said he supposed so. He said, "Brad was a hell of a good friend of mine."

Bill Weigand waited.

"We hit it off," Strothers said. "One of those things. I went after him for backing, first off. But I got fond of the big goof. Guess he did of me. You know how those things happen, sometimes?"

"Yes."

"Saw a lot of him. Used to go around with him — him and Phyllis, I and whoever turned up. That was before he fell for Nay, of course. Went on binges together, a few times. At his place, a good deal. Even went out to his Long Island place once or twice but, God, everybody talked about horses. Now and then, as a big concession, about dogs."

"He planned to marry Miss Shaw," Bill said. "Take her out of the play. That didn't make any difference?"

"That — " Strothers began, and said, "Wait a minute." He went back to the kitchenette and poured himself coffee from the bubbling percolator. He added cream. He looked at Bill Weigand, and Bill shook his head once more. Strothers brought his coffee back, and sat down facing Weigand.

"No," he said. "It didn't make any difference. Hell, who could blame him? Nay's a dish. But — she'd have stayed on in the show. All she had to do was to bring him around. Way he felt, he'd have done whatever she asked, in the end."

"And — she wanted to stay on?"

"Would have, when she thought about it. One thing about Nay, she's a trouper. At bottom. Take more than getting married to keep her off the stage. Hell — it did before."

"So you weren't worried?"

"No. I wasn't worried. Poor Sammy may have been. After all, he doesn't know much about show people. First time he's done a play, you know. Also — well, Sammy's an excitable sort of guy. You've seen that, haven't you?"

Bill nodded.

"Between us," Strothers said, "he's not very well balanced. All that finger snapping. Always imagining things." He shook his head. "Of course," he said, "Sammy's a writer. Never knew one that — " He shrugged to finish the sentence. He drank coffee. "Also," he said, "Sammy didn't know Brad. Brad didn't louse things up for people. Not that sort of guy. But Sammy didn't know him. Well?"

"One other thing," Bill said. "You were at this stag party Mr. Fitch gave before he died?"

"Sure," Strothers said. "On top of the world, poor Brad was."

"Mr. Wyatt was there?"

"For a while. As I remember it, he left early. Early as things go at that kind of binge."

"You stayed later?"

"A bit later."

"Mr. Fitch had been drinking a good deal?"

Strothers shook his head. This time he smiled.

"Probably," he said. "I didn't think about it at the time because — well, he just went along with the rest of us. I'm afraid I — lacked perspective."

"How about Mr. Wyatt?"

"I don't remember anything special. I suppose he'd had a few. Everybody had."

Bill Weigand left Mr. Strothers drinking coffee. He went back to his car and to Homicide East. Detective Willings waited for him.

Mr. and Mrs. James Nelson admitted readily that they had been at the apartment; agreed that they had probably arrived a short time before eight; agreed that, leaving, they had found the elevator without an operator and had, themselves, pushed the proper buttons. And — they had seen Mrs. Hemmins, alive and well, and had left her so.

Why had they gone?

They had got to talking, Mrs. Nelson said — then doing the talking for both of them. "He just sat there and nodded; almost went to sleep a couple of times," Willings reported.

They had got to talking about what they would do with that barn of a place, when they took it over.

"They seem pretty sure they're going to take over?"

"Yes sir. You mean they're not going to?"

"I'm afraid they're going to be disappointed, Freddy. Go ahead."

They had, Mrs. Nelson said, decided to go down and have a look at their prospective property — and problem. They had found Mrs. Hemmins, and she had taken them through the apartment. Followed by Toby, the cat. Mrs. Hemmins had been wearing a black dress.

"Very proper and everything," Mrs. Nelson told Willings, who not only spoke her language, but looked the part. "Only — "

Only — Mrs. Hemmins had looked several times at the watch on her wrist. "As if she wanted us to go. I supposed she was expecting someone. So we didn't stay long — just long enough to look around. Because I feel so strongly that people who *impose* on servants — "

"Write it out in the morning," Bill said, looking at his own watch.

He went home, then. He found Dorian, very lovely in a pale green negligee. He had time to kiss her once before the telephone rang.

Dogged would do it, Jerry North supposed. He would keep a stiff upper lip and his shoulder to the wheel — and his hand to the plow, for that matter — and even the weariest Braithwaite would wind somewhere safe to print. If only the man could, even once, encounter an infinitive without splitting it. From stem to stern. He was, he thought, beginning to think like Mr. Braithwaite. But thousands of readers were waiting. Braithwaiting. Jerry laid Page 342 face down and started on Page 343. Pam said something from the bedroom, where he had assumed her sleeping. Probably, wasn't he ever coming to bed? Probably, didn't he know it was past midnight?

Jerry had been writhing in one of Mr. Braithwaite's sentences, and Pam's words came to him dimly. He reached the end of the sentence and was conscious of a vague dissatisfaction. Not with Braithwaite — there was nothing vague about that. This was the slightly guilty consciousness of having missed something. Listening back, it did not feel as if Pam had said it was getting late, or even that, if he got no sleep, he would be no good the next day. It sounded —

Forget it, Jerry told himself. Now and then she says things to herself. For emphasis, probably. He stiffened his upper lip, and started the next sentence. "Ragweed." "*Rag*weed?"

There wasn't anything about ragweed in the sentence. Mr. Braithwaite's heroine was retreating up winding stone stairs, preparing for the — unsuccessful, if he knew Braithwaite — defense of her virtue in the tower room. There was nothing about ragweed in it. Why, then, had he suddenly thought, "Ragweed"? He —

Jerry North took off his glasses and laid them on the Braithwaite manuscript. He moved very carefully. He went out of his study and across the hall and to the open door of the bedroom.

Pam North was very wide awake. She was sitting up in bed. She looked at Jerry in some surprise.

"Pam." Jerry said. "You said something?"

"Did I?" Pam said. "I'm sorry, dear. I know I do sometimes. How is Mr. Braithwaite?"

Jerry gestured Braithwaite aside.

"Listen," he said, "did you say something about 'ragweed'? By any chance?"

"Ragweed?" Pam said. "What about ragweed. Oh, that. No, I don't think so. Anyway, I've got way past that, now. That was *hours* ago."

"Just a minute ago," Jerry said. "What about ragweed?"

"Goldenrod's better," Pam said. "More apposite. Because a field of goldenrod is really very pretty."

"Please," Jerry said. "Please, Pam."

"Oh, it's nothing," Pam said. "Or, actually, it's very obvious. Nobody hates goldenrod. Enough to kill it, I mean."

"I don't . . ." Jerry said. "Wait a minute. Ragweed! Goldenrod?" He almost snapped his fingers. "As a matter of fact," he said, "people do. Or try to."

"Not personally," Pam said. "What I mean is, you don't go out to a stalk of goldenrod and — and pull a knife on it. Say, 'That for you, goldenrod.' It isn't personal. It isn't as if he was afraid of them. They merely get in his nose. And sinuses, probably."

"Pam," Jerry said, and spoke very carefully. "You're talking about Wyatt? And cats?"

"Of course," Pam said. "I don't think you ought to try to read Mr. Braithwaite when you're so sleepy. What did you think I was talking about?"

Jerry went into the room. He sat on his bed and looked at Pam in hers. He steeled his mind against distraction.

"All right," he said. "Let's have it." She grinned at him. "With a straight face," he said.

"Sam is allergic to cats," Pam North said. "They give him symptoms. *But* — he isn't an ailurophobe. He doesn't hate them, as people who are uncontrollably afraid of them do. So, he wouldn't wantonly kill a cat. And Mrs. Hemmins' cat was killed wantonly."

"He may have attacked the murderer."

"Jerry!" Pam said. "And you a cat man! Oh, defending kittens, of course. But not defending people. We have to admit that."

"All right," Jerry said. "We have to admit that."

"Then," Pam said, "wantonly. But still — why? Because the cat was there — there and alive? A kind of sadism? That's too easy, isn't it? Or, because there's somebody else who's *really* a cat hater?"

"Well," Jerry said, "that's possible, isn't it?"

"Oh," Pam said. "Possible." Her tone dismissed it. "Anything's possible, I suppose. Or — because somebody wanted to put it on Sam Wyatt?"

"Well — " Jerry said. "As you say, anything's possible."

"Some things much more than others," Pam said. "Everybody who knows Sam knows about this allergy of his. And, most people think it *is* the same thing as ailurophobia. You know they do."

"I don't suppose most people think much about it one way or the other," Jerry said. "But — probably you're right."

"So," Pam said, "the murderer is some

233

woman who knows Mr. Wyatt, knows about this — ailment of his, and so killed the cat for good measure."

"Good measure? And — wait a minute. You said — "

"Mr. Wyatt had already found Mr. Fitch's body. He had a motive. Mrs. Hemmins had made this mistake about his having symptoms *before* she let him in the apartment. He's a little odd anyway. He's an ailurophobe. Ergo, he kills cats. That's what's supposed to be thought."

"Wait," Jerry said. "Please wait, Pam. Why a woman? And, why are you so sure Mrs. Hemmins made a mistake?"

"Because," Pam said, "a woman killed Mr. Fitch. *And* Mrs. Hemmins. Not Sam Wyatt."

Jerry ran a hand through his hair.

"Killing the cat is the last thing Sam would do, of course," Pam said, rather obviously making it all clear to a plodding mind. "Because it would point to him. So, if he didn't kill Mrs. Hemmins, Mrs. Hemmins made a mistake. I don't see how it could be any clearer."

"Because then he didn't kill Fitch?"

"Of course. Whoever killed Mr. Fitch killed Mrs. Hemmins. Because she had found the tea-towel."

"I'm not sure," Jerry said, "that Braithwaite

isn't easier. Not so — stimulating, perhaps."
He looked at her. "I speak purely of intellec-
tual stimulation, of course," he added.

"It's a great time to tell me," Pam said. She
clasped her hands behind her head.

"Perhaps I spoke too soon," Jerry said.
"Anyway — what about the tea-towel?"

"Wadded up," Pam said. "People get in
habits about them. Some people, when they've
finished with a tea-towel, and it's damp — from
wiping dishes, you know — "

"Yes," Jerry said. "I know, Pam."

"From hearsay," Pam said. "However —
some people would no more think of not hanging a damp towel up, carefully, to dry than
they'd think of flying through the moon. Other
people just wad them up and drop them somewhere. Because they're so glad the dishes are
done."

"A man might do that."

He still missed the point, Pam told him. Of
course a man might. Probably would. But, in
this case, it was an instance of an established
habit — something so habitual that it was instantly identifying. Had been to Mrs. Hemmins. Therefore, it was somebody who had
often been in the small serving pantry off
Fitch's quarters on the second floor of the duplex and, had often wiped dishes there and
had always wadded the tea-towel up. In other

words, a woman friend.

Jerry shook his head, but he shook it slowly.

"The only reason Mrs. Hemmins would have had the tea-towel in her hand," Pam said, "was to show it to someone. She did that only because it meant something. It wasn't a particularly interesting tea-towel; it meant something because it was wadded up. Is it clear so far?"

"I guess so," Jerry said.

"So — she found it in Mr. Fitch's little serving pantry after he was killed. Somebody had used it to — " She paused. "Well — " she said.

"Things had been cleaned up," Jerry said. "The tray the stuff was served on — to avoid fingerprints on the glass — had been washed. And dried, I suppose."

"That's it," Pam said. "I just couldn't think for a minute. She found it there — probably when Mr. Wyatt went to the lower floor to telephone the doctor — and it meant something to her. Meant — the identity of the murderer. She saved it and tried blackmail."

She waited. She said, "You see now, don't you, darling? Hell hath no fury."

"I suppose," Jerry said, "you mean Phyllis Barnscott? You've come round to her?"

"Oh," Pam said, "I started with her, really. As soon as I realized it wasn't Sam. Because, while I love Bill, of course, I thought it was mean of him to tease Dorian the way he did at the Algonquin."

Jerry ran a hand thoughtfully through his hair. He had thought Pam started with ragweed. Ragweed had come into it —

"So," Pam said, "I'm not stimulating any more?"

She could not, Jerry decided, be left under so absurd a misapprehension.

# XI

*Monday, 1:25 A.M. to 12:20 P.M.*

It had taken Bill Weigand some little time to get there. He had garaged his car, and had had to wait while a sleepy attendant was aroused, while the Buick came — with a kind of reluctance — down a spiraling ramp from the third floor. By the time Bill had driven to Naomi Shaw's small house, others of his trade almost filled the house. Mullins met him at the door.

"Hard to get anything out of her," Mullins said. "Not that she doesn't talk." He sighed. "Never heard anybody talk so fast."

Bill went ahead of Mullins into the living room. A uniformed sergeant stood in front of a woman of middle age, who had pale red hair, who wore a dark blue dressing gown, who talked and wept. "Yes'm," the sergeant said, and nodded. "That's right, ma'am. Don't you worry."

The sergeant turned to Weigand when Weigand reached them. "All worked up," the sergeant said. "Name's Blythe. Mrs. Nellie

Blythe. She's — "

" — forgive myself," Nellie Blythe said, and her plump hands fluttered. "Never. If I'd only — "

" — been going on like this ever since I got here. Maybe we ought to get a doctor."

They would see, Bill told him.

"Well," the sergeant said, "wish you luck, captain. You talk to the captain, now, ma'am. Tell him what happened."

"Nobody's *doing* anything," Nellie Blythe said, and put her hands over her eyes and swayed backward and forward on the straight chair she sat on. "The poor lamb'll be — oh dear, oh dear. In-a-trunk, like-as-not." Her speech was very rapid, and indistinct.

"Mrs. Blythe," Weigand said. He drew a chair up and sat in front of her. "Listen to me." She did not appear to hear him. "Mrs. *Blythe!*" he said, raising his voice. "You want to help, don't you?"

"The poor lamb," Nellie Blythe said. "The-poor-poor-lamb." But she looked at Bill Weigand. "Can't you do something?" she said. "Can't you do *any*thing?"

"I have to know what happened," Bill said. "Start at the beginning."

"I've told it over and over," she said. "Nobody *does* anything. At the bottom of the river by now, like as not. I'll never forgive myself — never. The pretty sweet thing and after all these years of taking care of her and her saying, 'I can't think what I'd do without you, Nellie dear,' and pressing out her pretty little dresses to say nothing of — "

The words ran together.

"Tell me what happened," Bill said. "Start at the beginning. What time was it?"

" — taking her breakfast in every morning and — what did you say?"

He leaned toward her. He said, very slowly, very carefully, "What time did this happen?"

"I looked at the clock," she said. "It was a quarter of one. When I first heard them. Shouting, he was, and threatening and — "

It took time. It took patience. Patience can be hard to maintain when one is tired; a story can be hard to get from a woman who is almost hysterical.

Naomi Shaw had come in before eleven that evening. She had come in alone. There had been nothing the waiting Nellie Blythe could do for her. She had seemed in good spirits. She had sent Mrs. Blythe to bed, and Mrs. Blythe had climbed the stairs to her room on the third floor, and undressed and gone to bed.

She had been awakened by raised voices, a man's dominant. The voices came from the living room below. She could not, at least at first, make out words. And, at first, she heard only the man's voice, not Naomi's. "Such a pretty soft voice she had, the lamb." At first, Nellie Blythe had felt no alarm.

"She'd let whoever it was in," she explained. "That's what I thought. I ought to have known. I'll never forgive — "

"There was no way you could have known," Bill told her. "No doubt she had done the same thing before."

"If you mean — " Mrs. Blythe said.

He meant nothing, he told her. Theater people keep late hours. They are gregarious. He meant only that.

"The sweetest lamb ever was," Mrs. Blythe said. "Whatever anybody says. I won't have anybody — "

"The voices kept you awake?"

That was it. At first she had merely assumed a somewhat noisy caller. Possibly some friend of Miss Nay's who had had a drink or two. She had turned over and tried to go back to sleep. It was possible that she had even dozed a little. But then, again, the voices had awakened her. This time the man had spoken so loudly.

" — *do what I tell you!*"

She had heard that very clearly. "He was shouting at her." And she had heard Naomi Shaw's answer. It had been, " — no good to yell at me."

There had been, then, a period during which the listening, by now frightened, woman two floors above could understand no words, although the man still shouted and Naomi Shaw still answered him, in a voice less violent, but still raised. "She was worked up, the poor lamb. That lovely voice of hers, but sometimes she got worked up. Oh dear! Oh dear!"

The plump hands began to flutter again.

"I'll never forgive — " she said.

"Mrs. Blythe!" Bill said. "Pull yourself together. What happened then?"

They had, apparently, merely kept on with it. "Him threatening. And I just laid there and — "

Once Naomi Shaw had said something about "waking the neighborhood." Once the man had said, " — can't get away with it, no use trying." And, somewhat later, Naomi had said, "No! I tell you — *no!* I — "

"It was like he'd grabbed her," Mrs. Blythe said. "Put his big hands on her pretty little neck. *Choked her!* So she couldn't finish what she started to say."

There had been silence, then. And the silence was more frightening than the shouted words had been. Then Mrs. Blythe had got out of her bed, and put her robe around her, and gone to the head of the stairs.

"Like I should have done at first. I'll never — "

"You heard nothing?"

"After a minute. Somebody slammed the door."

She called down, then; called, "Miss Nay? Are you all right, Miss Nay?" She had not been answered. She had hurried down the stairs, clutching the robe around her, calling to Naomi Shaw as she hurried down. And hearing no answer, hearing no sound.

"Lying there, all bloody. The poor, poor lamb," Mrs. Blythe said, and Bill Weigand, startled, said, "*What?*"

"I expected that," she said. "The poor lamb dead in her own blood. Or strangled, with her pretty face all black and ugly. Or — "

"But actually?" Bill said.

"She wasn't there. Nobody was there. The lights were on but — *there was nobody there!* Kidnapped. That's what it was. The poor lamb kidnapped. Taken some place and murdered, like as not. Crammed in a trunk, like they do. Or cement poured on her and dropped in the river."

"There's no reason to think that," Bill said. "Try not to be so excited, Mrs. Blythe."

"No reason," she said. "He says — *no reason!*" She looked imploringly at the ceiling. "Threatened by this great hulking beast. Kidnapped. Dragged out of her own home. And he says — "

"You didn't see the man. You couldn't have, could you?"

"Heard him," she said. "Hearing was plenty."

"But," Bill said, "not enough to show you he was a big man. A hulking man."

"I'll never forgive myself," Mrs. Blythe said. "Not if I live to be a hundred."

"You didn't recognize the voice? You probably know most of Miss Shaw's friends."

"He was shouting," she said. "How can you tell when people shout? Anyway, the voices come up through something. So they don't sound right." She paused. "Like one of those echo-chamber things," she said. "Oh dear, Oh dear!" She began to rock back and forth again.

Bill stood up. He beckoned the uniformed sergeant, asked him to see what he could do. Get her something to drink; if necessary, get a doctor to give her a sedative.

With Mullins, Bill checked the first floor. They found nothing that proved, or indeed, suggested, anything. They went through the rest of the house, and found nothing — no aftermath of violence, nothing. In closets on the second floor — closets off bedroom, and off dressing room — many pretty dresses hung prettily. In a small storage room a trunk and matched luggage had gathered a just perceptible film of dust.

"Nothing to get us anywhere," Mullins said, and added that, as he had said, it was a screwy one. "We put it on the tickers?"

They did, Bill agreed — and he, Mullins, could see to it.

Bill Weigand used the telephone. A bell in Wesley Strothers' downtown apartment rang unanswered. So did a bell in Samuel Wyatt's uptown apartment. At Robert Carr's hotel no bell was rung. Mr. Carr had checked out that afternoon.

By ten-thirty Monday morning, Acting Captain William Weigand had been at his desk for almost two hours. He had a slight headache. His eyes smarted. Deputy Chief Inspector Artemus O'Malley wanted to see him at eleven o'clock. It was, in all respects, a bad morning. Lack of sleep and superfluity of Inspector O'Malley were in themselves bad enough. But those things could be borne. Bill Weigand had borne them for some years.

The late editions of the morning newspapers were full of it. "Nay Shaw Snatched," the *Daily Mirror* announced on its front page, the three words occupying the front page. *The New York Herald Tribune* had found time to select, and front page space to print, a picture (in bathing suit) of Miss Naomi Shaw, star of

*Around the Corner,* mysteriously missing from her home after an apparent quarrel with an unidentified man. *The New York Times* reported that the police had sent out a nine-state alarm for Miss Naomi Shaw after they had been summoned to the house she occupied in East Sixty-second Street and found her maid in hysterics and Miss Shaw missing.

Considering the late hour at which the absence of the actress had been reported, journalistic enterprise had been extreme. The early editions of the afternoon papers would go to town on it. Inspector O'Malley would be displeased. Bill was displeased himself.

He had had the solution in his hands. It had been snatched away. It came to that. He had gone home after a long day's work and, as he drove through almost deserted streets, the solution had become obvious — so obvious that he wondered he could ever have been in doubt. All logic pointed in one direction, and if legal proof did not — well, legal proof would no doubt be forthcoming. It almost always was. But then the telephone had rung loudly in his apartment. He could still hear it ringing. And with the first words he had heard on the telephone, the logical structure had crumbled.

You could not, so far as he could now see, fit the kidnapping of Naomi Shaw into anything. He had spent most of the night trying to, while awake and while dreaming. He had worried at it while he drove to the office of Homicide East; it had nagged at him while he read accumulated reports, which had to do with the murders of Bradley Fitch and Rose Hemmins, but not with the disappearance of Naomi Shaw. On that, there was nothing. Bulletins had gone out over teletypes and, so far as results were concerned, fallen over the edge of the earth.

He had read a copy of Fitch's will, and found that it repeated what he knew. He had learned, from the report of a State policeman, that Mr. and Mrs. James Nelson had, that spring, discharged the full-time gardener they had employed for years, and that one three-acre piece of their considerable acreage, previously part of the expansive lawn, had been let go to meadow. It was even reported that Mrs. Nelson was doing some of her own cooking. Mr. Nelson had, for some months, been buying blended whiskey.

Mr. Wesley Strothers was at present in his apartment in a creaky building on Bank Street, and it was to be presumed that he was sleeping there, since he had got in about three in the morning. Where he had been from the time Bill left him, drinking coffee, presumably in for the night — although he had not said so — to the time of his belated return was anybody's guess. He had been gone when a detective arrived to keep vigil, which meant that he must have left his apartment shortly after Bill had left him.

The telephone rang. Sergeant Mullins answered it, listened, said, "Yeah. Thanks," and hung up.

Mrs. James Nelson had checked out of the Barclay at nine thirty-five. She had checked out for herself and her husband, but her husband had not been in evidence. She had got into a cab, with luggage, and been driven to Grand Central. She was now one of a small group waiting for the gates to open on the 10:55 New Haven local, due in Stamford at 12:01 — and at Rye, New York, at 11:41. Her husband was still not in evidence.

Mr. Arnold Latham, Jr., interviewed on a Long Island golf course late the afternoon before, had said he had not seen Bradley Fitch in months and hadn't wanted to see him. He said that, living or dead, Bradley Fitch was, to him, a heel of the first water. He had said that if they started bothering his sister he would see about it. He had said that she had had enough grief with that heel. He said that all he knew about Naomi Shaw was that she was in some show or other, and that he hadn't seen the show. How Mr. Latham had spent his evening and night was nobody's damned business. And he knew what his rights were.

Mr. Samuel Wyatt had gone from the Park Avenue apartment house, after Bill had interviewed him, to his hotel, and to his room. He had, so far as was known, remained in it — so far as was known. If he had had reason, he could have got out unseen and returned unseen. Perfect surveillance is not to be achieved, within the limits imposed by manpower.

The telephone rang.

Sergeant Mullins said, "Yeah." He said, "That's just dandy, Joe." To Weigand he said, "Mr. Wyatt has just had breakfast sent up to his room."

"That," Bill said, "is just dandy. Breakfast for one?"

"Joe didn't — " Mullins began, and then said, "Hey! You think that — "

"No, sergeant," Bill said. "I doubt if he's got Miss Shaw in his room."

Miss Phyllis Barnscott's movements had not been checked on since she had left the Algonquin the evening before, presumably to meet Mr. Jasper Tootle. Mr. Tootle had not yet been checked on at all. Mr. G. K. Snaith, artists' representative, had telephoned the police at a few minutes after nine that morning. He had wanted to know what things were coming to if a bunch of hoodlums could kidnap a girl like Naomi Shaw — "an *artist*" —

right from under their noses. He had been asked whether he had any suggestions. His only suggestion had been that they'd better find her, pronto.

Mr. Snaith owned ten per cent of her, Bill thought. He probably regarded her kidnapping as a form of grand larceny.

Mr. Robert Carr, after checking out of his hotel, had vanished. It was possible that he had returned to Chicago. It was also possible, of course, that he had returned to Pakistan. But when he heard of the disappearance of his former wife, he would probably return. With, Bill Weigand thought, bells on. He —

The telephone rang.

Sergeant Mullins said it was Mullins speaking. He said, "Yes'm, he is." He said, "Do you now?" He said, "Well, I am. In a manner of speaking." He held a hand over the transmitter and said, "Mrs. North. She says she knows who killed 'em. She says I'm very Irish this morning."

Bill took the telephone. In spite of himself, his voice sounded weary. He could hear the weariness, the depression, in his own voice.

"Jerry and I talked about it all night," Pam North said. "Well, most of the night. What's the matter with you, Bill?"

"Nothing," Bill Weigand said. "I was up most of the night too. About the murders?"

"Of course," Pam said. "Although mostly about the tea-towel. Then we saw how it had to be."

"Both of you?"

"Well — in the end. At first Jerry kept thinking about Mr. Braithwaite. Do you ever read Braithwaite?"

"No," Bill said.

"I keep telling Jerry that," Pam said. "But he shows sales figures. About the murders. It had to be a woman, of course. But probably you've already seen that. *Please*, Gin!"

Bill had not. He said he had not. He was told why it had to be a woman. He said, "Well — " There was also the matter of the cat, sacrificed to throw suspicion on Samuel Wyatt. "Well — " Bill said.

"You don't," Pam said, "seem as interested as I'd hoped. Coals to Newcastle?"

"What? Oh — I had thought about the tea-towel. You're probably right that she was showing it to the man who killed her. Quite possibly because it had been, as you say, wadded up. And — "

"Man?" Pam said. "But that's the whole point. Men don't. I mean, not enough for it to be a habit. What I mean is — "

"I know," Bill said.

"And as for the cat," Bill said. "Did you ever think of a double frame?"

"I don't — oh. You mean Mr. Wyatt could have framed himself? So we'd think he'd been? But isn't the trouble with that that we mightn't notice he *had* been? I mean in the first place?" She paused. "I make it sound very complicated, don't I? And you're tired already. Wait — has something else happened?"

"Haven't you read the papers, Pam?"

"Of course," Pam said. *"Bill! It hasn't started?"*

It was a comment on the world they lived in that this needed no interpretation. Bill said it had not started; he said that, if it did, it was unlikely they would need newspapers to tell them so. He said, "Do you get the latest editions?"

"No," Pam said. "I don't see why, either. When we live right here in New York. Often as not, we don't get Mr. Atkinson until the next day. What was in the late editions?"

He told her. She said, "Oh." She said, "No wonder you're tired." There was a long pause.

"It doesn't fit, does it?" Pam said. "She's sure it was a man? The maid, I mean?"

She was quite sure, Bill told her.

"Of course," Pam said, "she was on the third floor. She was half asleep."

"A man. Shouting."

"Phyllis Barnscott has a very deep voice. Almost baritone sometimes."

252

"Still, I doubt it."

There was a longer pause.

"I thought I had it all worked out," Pam North said.

"So did I, as a matter of fact."

There was surprise in Pam's voice, then. She said she couldn't see what it did to Bill's theory. Hers — yes. Unless they wanted a co-incidence. But his — he already thought it was a man.

"Mine too," Bill said. "Because, as you say, it doesn't fit in. The point is — mine was the wrong man. The whole point having been — " He stopped. Something had flickered in his mind; flickered out again.

"Are you still there?" Pam said. "Or have you just gone to sleep?"

But Sergeant Mullins was leaning across the desk. Sergeant Mullins was pointing at his wrist watch. It showed ten minutes of eleven; Deputy Chief Inspector Artemus O'Malley was in his office in West Twentieth Street. In ten minutes, Deputy Chief Inspector Artemus O'Malley would begin to wait. Inspector O'Malley was not good at waiting.

"I've got to go," Bill said. "Got to see Art — the inspector."

"No!" Pam said. "When you're tired already!"

"Pam," Bill said. "Don't go off on your own,

will you? This time?"

"With you so tired already?" Pam said. "And Jerry to his ears in Braithwaite? Would I be likely to?"

Bill was only partly reassured. But there was no time. . . .

Sirens on police cars are supposed to be used only in emergency. But Inspector O'Malley, in the minds of Sergeant Mullins and Acting Captain Weigand, constitutes a permanent emergency. The Buick snarled at traffic on Park Avenue, at traffic on Fourth. Traffic patrolmen shrilled whistles for it, and held up hands. Mullins drove.

It was something he had heard, Bill thought. Something he had heard, and not taken in. Something that cleared up the whole problem, made it fit again as it had fitted the night before, made it —

"Well," Bill said. *"I'll be damned!"*

There was no longer weariness in his voice.

Mullins, turning right off Seventh Avenue into West Twenty-first, did not take his eyes from the roadway. But he said, "O.K., Loot?"

"Right," Bill Weigand said. "O.K. I think, sergeant. I'm pretty sure it is."

They were three minutes late at Inspector O'Malley's office, and so had only to wait a quarter of an hour for Inspector O'Malley. Waiting, Bill Weigand was restless. That way again, Sergeant Mullins thought. Shouldn't be long now.

They listened to Inspector O'Malley. They said, "Yes sir. That's right, sir." They were models of policemen listening to an inspector of police. They were told that it was their baby, and that O'Malley couldn't do everything, and that they were young cops, with a lot to learn. They were told not — for God's sake not — to let the Norths mess it up. They were told to get on with it — and permitted, after only forty-five minutes, to do so. They drove back, quietly, to the office.

Samuel Wyatt sat on a bench; sagged on the bench. His clothes seemed, more than ever, too large for him. As Bill Weigand and Mullins went through the squad room of Homicide East a detective on duty there jerked his head toward Wyatt, said, "Man wants to see you, captain." Bill crossed the room and stood in front of Wyatt, who regarded the dusty floor. After waiting a moment, Bill said, "Yes, Mr. Wyatt?"

Sam Wyatt looked up, then, as if he had been suddenly awakened. He snapped fingers on both hands, simultaneously. He said, "This last meal. The one they can choose. Do they actually eat it?"

"Sometimes, I suppose," Bill said. "I don't really know, Mr. Wyatt."

"Haven't you ever wondered?"

255

"Yes," Bill said, "I've wondered. I don't think about it much."

"Although you've sent people there."

"Probably that's the reason," Bill said. "You wanted to see me?"

"I've been sitting here trying to imagine it," Wyatt said. "Feel how it would feel. What a man would order. I've read that a good many of them order roast chicken. Or steak. You'd think it would be something strange, wouldn't you? Some unfamiliar food they had always wondered about. Escargots, perhaps. Have you ever eaten them, captain?"

"Yes," Bill said. "I've eaten them. They're very good."

"I never have," Wyatt said. "I've been trying to think why. Did you ever have a manicure? A professional one, I mean."

"No," Bill said.

"Neither have I," Wyatt said. He snapped his fingers. "Well," he said. There was a certain finality about it. It was almost, Bill thought, as if now, with these things settled, he might get up and leave.

"You wanted to see me," Bill said.

"You probably think I'm nuts," Wyatt said. "Or — pretending to be nuts. For future reference."

"I hadn't thought that," Bill said. "Come in the office."

256

They went into a small inner office, which was entirely utilitarian, the window of which needed washing. Bill sat at his desk and Wyatt sat opposite him. Wyatt snapped his fingers several times.

"You want to make another statement?" Bill asked him.

Wyatt looked at Sergeant Mullins, sitting at a smaller desk with a notebook in front of him. He looked back at Bill Weigand. He snapped his fingers once more.

"Somebody," Wyatt said, "is trying to frame me." He looked at Weigand very intently. "I suppose that's an old story," he added.

"I've heard it before."

"Wasn't it ever true?"

"Sometimes. Not often, Mr. Wyatt."

"It is this time. I've been thinking it over — walking the streets and thinking it over. That's the only answer. That's why Mrs. Hemmins was killed. Because I had a motive for killing her. To stop her from repeating her story that I 'had a cold' when she let me in."

"You denied that," Bill said. "So — it would have been your word against hers. You pointed that out, you know."

"All right," Wyatt said. "Only — she was telling the truth. She'd have made people — feel she was telling the truth. That's supposed to be my motive."

"Then you had been in the apartment earlier?"

"He was dead already. I realized nobody would believe — "

"Mr. Wyatt," Bill said. "Why are you telling us this? Now?"

"Because," Wyatt said, "I wouldn't kill her to keep her from telling what happened and then come to you and tell it myself."

"So, since you are telling us, you didn't kill her? And, if you didn't kill her, you didn't kill Fitch?"

"You can see that," Wyatt said. "I couldn't see any other way. It all — all kept piling up. The way it was planned to pile up."

"All right," Bill said. "Keep on telling us."

"He was dead before I got there. I got in a panic. I could see the way it would look, imagine what you people would think. I — I imagine things very clearly."

"Very," Bill said. "Go on, then."

Wyatt went on. As he did so, he snapped his fingers often. As he did so, he talked more rapidly, so that Mullins' quick pencil darted; so that, once or twice, Mullins said, "Hold it a minute. What was that?"

Saturday morning Wyatt had gone to Fitch's apartment — to Fitch's rooms on the second floor of the duplex — to make another appeal, to try once more to persuade Bradley Fitch to arrange somehow so that Naomi Shaw would remain in *Around the Corner*. "We had thought of some new arguments. He'd said, O.K., he'd listen. That was the night before.

"You think it was just because of the money coming in," Wyatt said. "It was more than that. It was — hell, all those people laughing. At *my* play." He snapped his fingers then. "Can't make an outsider understand that," he said. "All the same, that was part of it. I don't say all. Part."

He had rung the upstairs bell. It had not been answered. He had tried a second time. Then he had tried the knob of the door, and the knob had turned.

"Don't know why I did," he said. "Instinctive, I guess. I wanted to see him pretty bad. Maybe I thought he was asleep and — anyway, that's what I did."

The door had opened. It had opened enough so that, without entering the room, Sam Wyatt could see Fitch lying on the floor, could see the evidence of his final, violent illness. "I thought there was blood in it," Wyatt said.

"There was," Bill said. "He hemorrhaged. That's why he died so quickly. You didn't go into the room? See if you could do anything for him?"

He had, Wyatt said, started to leave without going into the room. But then he had decided he could not do that, and had gone in. He had felt for a heartbeat.

"He was dead," Wyatt said.

"You can't tell that easily," Bill told him. "Perhaps — never mind. You decided he was dead. Then?"

Then he had gone out and closed the door. And then —

"I thought, suppose it turns out somebody killed him? Nobody'll believe I wasn't the one. I'd better get out of here. I wiped the doorknob and then — then I thought, somebody'll have seen me coming up. The doorman or somebody. So — "

He had, he said, "plotted it out." Someone might have seen him enter the building, and even go into the elevator. But — nobody could tell whether he had gone to the ninth floor or the eighth. "There's no indicator on the elevator," he said.

"No," Bill said.

Instead, therefore, of leaving the building, as he had first thought of doing, Wyatt had gone down one floor and rung the bell there; had, with Mrs. Hemmins, found Fitch's body for the second time.

"If I was wrong about his being dead the first time," Wyatt said, "we were there again in — oh, in a few minutes. So if there had been any chance — But he was dead when I first saw him."

"All right," Bill said. "So that's — "

"It was that cat," Wyatt said. "There was no sign of a cat up there. Then, just before she let me in, it hit me. Otherwise, she wouldn't have said anything to make you believe I had been there before — you did believe that, didn't you?"

"Oh, yes," Bill said. "I believed that, Mr. Wyatt."

Wyatt nodded. He snapped his fingers. But, he said, he had gone too far to turn back. He had to bluff it out. Particularly after he had lied once, nobody would believe that he had not lied completely.

"I was a damned fool," he said. "What it comes to, I got myself into it by trying to get out."

"If you didn't kill Fitch," Bill said.

"I didn't. Doesn't my telling you this prove it?"

"No," Bill said. "Think it over. Carry it another step."

"I don't — " Wyatt began. But then he said, "That would be ingenious, I suppose. To tell why I'm supposed to have killed the poor old girl to keep her from telling, to prove I didn't kill her." He snapped his fingers. "I'm not that ingenious," he said.

"Aren't you?"

"All right," Wyatt said. "You think I'm lying both times. Well — it was a chance I had to take." He shrugged. "I wonder," he said, "if anybody ever *did* ask them for escargots?" He waited. "Well?" he said.

"I don't know," Bill said. "Mr. Wyatt, between the time Mrs. Hemmins heard the upstairs doorbell and the time she let you in downstairs, half an hour elapsed. And — when she heard the doorbell upstairs, she also heard someone — presumably Mr. Fitch — walk across the study to answer the bell. But, you say Fitch was already dead. And — you say you were there only a few minutes."

Wyatt shook his head sadly, hopelessly. He snapped his fingers. But then he brightened, and snapped his fingers again.

"That was whoever killed Brad," he said. "She — " He lost confidence again. "I guess she didn't hear the bell when I rang it."

"Why? If she heard it one time, why not the other?"

"It's no use, is it?" Wyatt said. "I told you what happened, but it's no use."

"You can't explain why she would hear the bell one time and not the other?"

Despondently, Wyatt shook his head.

"Unless," he said, "she was making a noise herself. Or — when I rang was somewhere she couldn't hear the bell."

"Where?"

"How would I know?" Wyatt said, and spoke hopelessly. "I don't know the layout."

Mullins looked at Bill Weigand and seemed about to speak. Bill shook his head, just perceptibly.

"About Mr. Strothers having been there yesterday evening," Bill said. "You were right about that."

Wyatt nodded dully, without interest.

"He went to ask Mrs. Hemmins if she wanted to work for him. When he moves in the fall. He says she was all right when he left."

"Sure," Wyatt said. "I supposed it was something like that."

"This stag party," Bill said. "The one Fitch gave the night before he was killed. You say you left early?"

"Yes."

"Why?"

"Why? I got bored, I suppose. What's that got to do with anything?"

He was not answered. Instead, Bill said, "All right, Mr. Wyatt. Thanks for coming in."

Wyatt looked at him in, apparently, complete surprise.

"You mean I can go?" he asked, and seemed incredulous.

"Right," Bill said. "Not too far. Where will

you be this afternoon?"

Strothers, Wyatt said, had called a rehearsal. To tighten up a couple of scenes. To "keep the boys and girls up to it." Wyatt said he supposed he would be at the theater. He stood up, but tentatively, as if he expected to be pulled down. He moved toward the door. He put a hand, doubtfully, on the knob.

"I take it," Bill Weigand said, "that you didn't read the newspapers this morning?"

Wyatt stopped, turned, looked more puzzled than he had before. Then he shook his head. "My God," he said, "I've got enough to worry about. Anyway, there wasn't an opening last night."

He waited.

"I hadn't realized that," Bill said. "Run along, Mr. Wyatt. We'll be seeing you."

Wyatt went.

"Loot," Mullins said, "Mrs. Hemmins went back into the servants' quarters after she heard Fitch stirring around — after she heard the bell ring. To wait for the servants' buzzer. If the upstairs bell rang again, maybe she wouldn't hear it. Maybe she was banging things around."

"Right," Bill said.

"Funny, Wyatt didn't think to bring that up."

"No," Bill said. "Not very. He's not supposed to know the layout, remember. He's said that. He can't suddenly know it now, to get himself off a hook."

Mullins nodded, thoughtfully, to that. He said, "Another thing, Loot-I-mean-captain. You figure he doesn't really know about the Shaw babe?"

Bill was drumming, lightly, on his desk with the tips of his fingers. He said it was possible.

"And Strothers doesn't? Don't any of them read the papers?"

Bill imagined that Strothers knew.

"Then what's the point of this rehearsal?"

"There can be two points," Bill said, and still spoke abstractedly, still looked at the opposite wall, and spoke as much to himself as to Mullins. "One, he knows Miss Shaw will be back. Two, he's decided he can get along without her. Put somebody else in. Like Miss Barnscott, for example."

Mullins thought for a time. He said it was all screwier than ever. The telephone interrupted him. He said, "Mullins speaking," and handed the telephone to Weigand.

"Right," Weigand said, after he had listened for a moment. "Ask her to come in, will you?" There was another moment. "Yes," he said. "Both of them, of course."

Weigand and Mullins watched the door. It was only a matter of seconds. Naomi Shaw came through it first.

# XII

*Monday, 1:30* P.M. *to 2:25* P.M.

Pamela North and Dorian Weigand sat in the last row of the orchestra of the Forty-third Street Theater, their backs to the barrier. They were waiting to ask Phyllis Barnscott whether she had murdered Bradley Fitch, and afterward Mrs. Rose Hemmins and whether, subsequently, she had arranged the kidnapping of Naomi Shaw. "Although," Pam had said, "I don't really think that. The other things, yes. Because she knew Mr. Fitch had hangovers, having been with him so much and probably, when you come down to it, in the mornings. And she would be the one to get breakfasts and clean up afterwards and that explains the tea-towel."

Dorian had said, "Well — " to this. She had said it several times, first on the telephone when she had been invited — urged — to accompany Pam when things were put up to Phyllis. "Because," Pam had explained, "I promised Jerry, *and* Bill, or as good as, that I wouldn't go off on my own this time, and if

266

you're with me, I'm not, am I?" Dorian had noted that this was somewhat specious but had then added that it would be very pleasant to have it turn out Phyllis Barnscott. "Because, frankly," Dorian had said, "she's a patting blonde."

They had not found the bright, blond actress at the Algonquin, as they had hoped. But there they had encountered Jasper Tootle, finishing an early lunch, and from him learned that Phyllis had been summoned to rehearse. "Taking advantage of the layoff to tighten up some scenes," Jasper had explained, but had shaken his handsome head over it, and admitted he didn't know precisely why. "With Nay God knows where," he had added.

They had found a sign in front of the theater which told them "No Performance Tonight" and had found the lobby empty and, although one of the ticket windows open, no one behind the grille to question their entrance. They had found their way in; it appeared that anyone who cared to could find his way, this Monday afternoon, into a theater which, only a few days before, had spilled over. They had taken the first seats they had come to, since it had been instantly apparent that they would have to wait before they could charge Phyllis Barnscott with murder.

The curtain was up and light glared on the

stage. It glared from a single, powerful bulb on a standard, a little to the right of stage center, as they looked at it from the auditorium. There were people on the stage, in the glare. There were also, less brightly lit, people in the orchestra seats. A flight of temporary wooden stairs ran up from the orchestra to the stage. A tall, slightly stooped man was standing with his back to the light, talking to those on the stage, but with his voice raised to carry to others in the seats.

" — all stick around," he said. "The assumption we're going on is, she'll get back. Be found — get back somehow. If she doesn't — O.K., we've wasted time. If she does, we've rubbed the rust off, and there's a hell of a lot of rust. O.K.?"

Nobody said anything. The light on the stage reached only a little way into the auditorium; beyond its limit the shadows deepened. Here and there in the shadows, cigarettes glowed. There seemed, indeed, to be a good many people in the theater, scattered widely, but for the most part in the rows closer to the stage. But at one side, well back, a cigarette glowed and diminished, glowed again. And halfway back, on the other side of the house, there were two dark figures, sitting side by side.

"O.K., then," Wesley Strothers said, and came down the wooden steps, his heels clattering on them. He sat in a center aisle seat in the fifth row, across the aisle from a man who, to Pam and Dorian, was a bald head attached — but how was not apparent — to a hand which held a cigarette. "Get on with it when you're ready, Marv," Strothers said.

Phyllis Barnscott was on the stage. (It had been on seeing her there, evidently inaccessible for the time, that Pam and Dorian had sat to wait.) The red-haired Jane Lamont was on the stage, and Sidney Castle, the leading man. They stood now, near the footlights, and looked down at the bald-headed man, who said they would take it from the telephone scene. "Gabble, gabble, gabble and what not and Pudgy wouldn't," Mr. Marvin Goetz, director of *Around the Corner*, said in a tired voice. "And try to get something *in* it. All right, get it set up."

Miss Barnscott left through a door at stage left. Miss Lamont — who wore slacks and a yellow blouse — went upstage to a chair and table, sat on the one and lifted a telephone from the other. She put the telephone in her lap. Castle stood near by and looked dourly down at her.

"For God's sake, Sid," Goetz said. "Can't you see you're screening her?" Castle moved back and to a side a step or two. "Last Tuesday night you were catching flies," Goetz said.

"I don't know how," Castle said.

"Pushing that damn handkerchief into your pocket, pulling it out again. That's how. Doing takes."

"Well," Castle said, "I can't just stand here."

"You can damn well try," Goetz said. "All right. Lisa says and so forth and so forth and — "

"Do you want the line?" Jane Lamont said.

"The cue, sweetheart," Goetz said, in a tone of inexpressible weariness. "Just the cue. Get the beat anyway you want. Now."

"Yackety yackety yackety and the rest of it," Jane Lamont said into the telephone, and as she said this Castle's handsome, but previously rather sullen, face was radiant with delight, "and Pudgy wouldn't."

"Tell him — " Castle said.

The door, stage left, through which Phyllis Barnscott recently had gone began to vibrate. It did not open. "Damn thing's stuck again," Phyllis, behind it, said angrily to anyone who would listen. "Why nobody — " The door opened suddenly. Miss Barnscott seemed to have been propelled through it.

"We'll get it fixed," Goetz said. "Billy? Where the hell's Billy?"

"All right, Mr. Goetz," a young man said, appearing part way through an obviously

270

practical window, stage right. "Get on it right away."

"Don't quite close it this time," Goetz said, to Phyllis Barnscott. "All right. From the same place."

"Yackety yackety yackety and the rest of it," Jane said into the telephone, and Castle's face burst into a smile.

"Tell him — " Castle began, through the smile, and Phyllis came through a door which, this time, opened — and was left open.

"Too *fast,*" Goetz said in a tone of anguish. "A beat too — go ahead. Go *ahead!*"

"Don't tell me you're trying it *again!*" Phyllis said, in a tone that bubbled. "Because if you — is that the way you want it, Marvin. Or, 'Don't tell *me?*' "

"*Sweetheart,*" Marvin Goetz said, threateningly. "I love you. We all love you. Why would it be 'Don't tell *me?*' What do you think it means?"

"I haven't the faintest idea," Phyllis Barnscott said. "I never have had. Mr. Wyatt? Are you out there, Mr. Wyatt?"

"Oh, God," Sam Wyatt said, from a shadowed seat off the right aisle — a seat two rows in front of two dark figures in adjacent seats. "Do we go through that again?"

"Now, Sammy," Goetz said. "Tell the pretty lady. Just once more."

271

"And," Phyllis said, "why the beat's wrong. Tell me that, darling. I've got to come clear over to her, don't I? And the way it is I'm just here" — she moved back a step, and stabbed at the floor with a heel — "when I get to 'again.' And look where I've got to get."

"Hold it a beat," Goetz said. "Two beats, if you need them."

"And she's saying it *again*," Wyatt said. "Not to you again, particularly. I'd think — "

Wesley Strothers stood up. He walked up the center aisle, and turned to cross behind the barrier. As he walked, he shook his head.

"Try it again, darlings," Goetz said.

"Yackety yackety yackety and the rest of it," Jane Lamont said, and Castle smiled again, and Phyllis, who had returned to the open door, but this time not through it, stepped into the living room ("Which so perfectly sets the tone of this delightful comedy" — John Chapman in the *Daily News*) and said, after holding it a beat, "Don't tell *me* you're trying *again* to — "

"Dorian," Pam North said, in a tight whisper. "Beyond the door. That's *Mullins!* Surely that's Mullins. And — "

But she stopped, because at that moment the French doors upstage parted and Miss Naomi Shaw stepped through them. She wore a white sports dress, and her soft hair was

272

held back from her face by a ribbon. She stood with her back to the doors, her hands, held behind her, touching them delicately.

"There's no use going on with — all this," she said, in her cadenced voice. "I'm so dreadfully sorry, but I'm afraid there isn't any use at all." She shook her shining head, slowly, tenderly. She turned a little toward the doors she had just parted, so that now the beautiful — as someone had said, the "lilting" — line of throat and chin was accented. "Come, darling," she said. "Come and help me tell these dear, *dear* people. Because — it's so dreadfully hard."

There was movement in the right aisle. It was the movement of the tall figure of Wesley Strothers down it. He walked down until he reached the seat from which Wyatt had spoken. He stood beside the dark blot which was Sam Wyatt.

Robert Carr came through the French doors. He blinked slightly in the glare from the unshaded bulb. He seemed a little embarrassed. Naomi moved — she seemed to flow — to the right so that he stood beside her.

"Robert married me this morning," Naomi Shaw said, with the simplicity which many consider the essence of art. "We found we just couldn't — "

("I *knew* it," Pam North said to Dorian, in a whisper. "I *knew* it was a love scene. Be-

273

cause kidnappers don't shout at their work, of course. It would be so — ")

" — drove to that dear little town in Delaware," Naomi said, and now she moved downstage a little, leaving Carr by the doors. He stayed there for a second. Then he moved to his left, away from the glaring light. He stood there, a square, solid man with a square brown face — and somewhat the air of a man who wishes something were over.

"He simply made me," Naomi said. "But really, it was that he made me *see*. See how wrong we were before to let little things — " The break was unconscious, was tremulous. The break was a refinement of the actor's craft. "When there could never be anyone else," she said. "Not for either of us."

"Well I'll be damned," Marvin Goetz said, and stood up in his seat. "I'll be eternally — "

"Marvin," Naomi said. "Dear Marvin. Oh — I love you all. This is so — so hard for me." There were tears in her soft, her indescribable, voice. "Please understand. *Please?* It is bigger than both of us." She paused at that, for an instant. "It's so hard to get the words right," she said, and smiled, disarmingly. "I'm not good at words. Not like you are, Sam — are you out there, Sam?"

"Oh," Sam Wyatt said from his seat, "I'm here all right."

"Your lovely play," Nay said. "But — you can get someone else. It won't be hard, really. Jane — dear Jane. Or — or Phyllis. Or someone? That's true, isn't it, Wes? Tell them it's true, so I won't feel such a — such a — traitor."

There was no answer to this. The silence was complete. Marvin Goetz sat down again. Naomi lifted a slender hand, as if to push back — as in the play she so often did — her softly heavy hair. But one could only suspect that she had forgotten the hair was now held back, so smoothly did the gesture become the gentle touching of her right temple. Naomi had — and Pam was surprised to notice this, so subtle had been the movement — moved forward, so that now she was close to the footlight trough.

"I so want you to understand," Naomi said, and by implication, if not in fact, reached out her hands toward those scattered in the seats in front of her. Phyllis, Jane Lamont and Castle were in a group, not far from the practical window. Robert Carr, who now had put his hands in his jacket pockets, stood alone, upstage and to the left. It was, Pam thought, as if, symbolically as well as in fact, the people of the theater had withdrawn from him, as from a pariah. "So *hope* you will understand," Naomi Shaw — no, now Naomi Carr once again — said, in the softest (and most hope-

275

ful) of tones. "It's always been Robert and me. From so many years ago, when we were growing up together, so far away from — all this." "All this" was identified, apparently as everything in front of her, by the most graceful of gestures.

"We didn't always realize," Naomi said. "I thought — you all know I thought — I could find someone else. Dear Brad — poor dear Brad. I was so fond of him but — but it wasn't the same. And then Robert came back to me."

She had her audience, now. There could be no doubt of that. (*But why*, Pam thought, *does she need all this?* She's hinted, not quite said. It's as if — as if she were deliberately building it. But she must, Pam decided, be wrong in that, for why would she?)

"And then," Naomi said, "Robert heard he had to go to — it's Pakistan, isn't it, dear?" She turned slightly toward Robert Carr.

"Chile," Carr said. His voice seemed flat after hers, downright.

"Of course," she said. "Chile, of course. He heard it last night and — and he came to me. He has to go — it is tomorrow, isn't it, darling?"

"Yes," Carr said.

"And then I knew," Naomi said. "Knew nothing else mattered. Not even my lovely play. Knew I had to go with him — Where he went I had to go. Always — that nothing else —"

Marvin Goetz stood up again.

"*Sweetheart!*" he said, and said it as an oath. "You're walking out on us? Just like —"

There was a shot, and the explosion roared in the theater. A rather large chunk of plaster fell out of the proscenium arch. Carr, in a movement like a cat's, threw himself to one side. Mullins came through the door at stage left with a revolver in his hand, and Bill Weigand came through the French doors, down to Naomi. He pushed her aside, toward the group at her right. Somewhere there was sudden, violent shouting; somewhere, behind the barrier against which Pam and Dorian sat, there was the noise of men hurrying. A door banged somewhere.

These things did not happen in sequence, but at once. And the house lights came on.

Two men were struggling in the aisle at the right. The taller shouted, "*No you don't. Not again!*" and they went down together, on the floor between the seats.

Mullins ran across the stage and down the wooden stairs. And two men who had been sitting very near in the darkness came out of their seats.

The struggling men rolled in the aisle. The taller man, who was on top, forced the hand of the smaller slowly upward, apparently against desperate resistance. And, between the two hands, clasped in struggle, there was an automatic pistol.

*"Got it!"* Wesley Strothers said, gasping a little from his effort. "Just in — "

Mullins reached them first. He wrenched the automatic from the hand that held it, pulled Strothers off Sam Wyatt. Wyatt, for a moment, lay on his back on the floor, and made no effort to get up. One of the men who had been sitting close pulled him to his feet.

"Oh God," Sam Wyatt said. "Oh God, oh God, oh *God!*"

"Hit anybody?" Strothers said, his voice still high, excited. "Carr all right?"

"Quite all right," Bill Weigand said, and then Pam saw, and Dorian saw, that Bill had not moved from where he stood near the footlights, at the center of the stage. "Nobody was hit. The shot went very wild."

"Thank God for that," Strothers said. "I was afraid for a moment I wouldn't be able — " He did not finish.

"You may as well come up here, Mr. Strothers," Bill said. "You too, Wyatt."

But Strothers had already started down the aisle. Wyatt came with Mullins' hand — the hand which did not hold the automatic — hard on his arm. Sam Wyatt kept shaking his head,

278

like a man who has been struck hard, is dazed by the blow. (Even now, Pam thought, I'm sorry for him. But how — ?)

Strothers went up the wooden stairs; Wyatt was propelled after him. Naomi Shaw was across the stage, held tight against Carr, who was watching with his face intent, his eyes narrowed. Facing Weigand, Strothers began to speak.

"When she said she was going with him," Strothers said. "Leaving the play. I'd been standing there, listening, and — and Sam moved. I felt him move, more than saw him. Then I looked and he'd got this gun out and was aiming at Carr. Then I jumped him, but the gun went off before I could stop it." He turned, abruptly, to Sam Wyatt. "You're crazy," he said. "You've gone crazy, Sam."

"It's no use," Wyatt said, in a dull voice. "All the time, I knew it wasn't any use." He turned, then, to face Strothers squarely. "Always a jump ahead, weren't you?" he said, and his voice was no longer dull. His voice vibrated with hatred. "A smart louse, Strothers. For the kind of louse you are. Want to know what kind?"

Sam Wyatt told the tall, dark-eyed producer — told him in crude, hard words.

Pam North expected Bill Weigand to interrupt. But he did not interrupt. He let Wyatt finish. Wesley Strothers listened, his face unchanged. Then Strothers shook his head, pityingly.

"That was the way it happened, then?" Bill said, when Wyatt had finished telling Strothers what kind of a louse he was. "You don't deny it happened that way?"

Bill's voice was even, unexcited. But there was an odd quality in it. Dorian Weigand clutched Pam's arm as she heard Bill speak. "Listen," she said. "When he talks that way — "

Apparently the odd note in Weigand's voice reached Wyatt's ears, as well. He looked at Weigand, and then his face began slowly to change.

"Do I need to?" he said, and waited. Weigand made a just perceptible motion with his head — a motion to which Mullins responded — before he answered. Then Bill Weigand said, "No, Mr. Wyatt. You don't need to."

Strothers whirled. And Mullins, behind him, took him by both arms. For an instant, it seemed that Strothers would try to break the big detective's grasp. But then he stood quiet, unresisting.

"I tell you," Strothers said, "he tried to kill — "

"No," Bill said. "Oh, it might have worked. Except — I already knew, Strothers. And so,

I was waiting for it. For something like it."

He turned away, then. He turned toward Naomi, who was still circled by Carr's arms.

"Was it all right?" Naomi asked.

"It was very good, Mrs. Carr," Weigand said. "Very good indeed."

"Oh," Naomi said. "I really can act, captain. I'm quite good, really."

# XIII

*Monday, 6:30 P.M. and after*

Bill had promised to drop by for a drink, when he could and if he could. Pam had taken Dorian home with her, more or less as a hostage. "Because," Pam said, "he must have known all the time, or at least for part of the time. And I thought Sam Wyatt and then Phyllis Barnscott, and he's got to tell me why I was so wrong."

"It's possible," Jerry said, stirring, "that you're slipping." He shook his head, elaborately. He said, "Tut, tut," in a tone of commiseration. He was, almost at once, disturbed to feel that Pam took seriously what was not seriously intended. "You were right about some of it," he said. "You were right about the cat. And, basically, about the tea-towel."

"I didn't come out right," Pam said. "There's no use trying to cheer me up. Of course, maybe I'll feel better after a drink, but that will just be a feeling, won't it? Just an illusion."

Martini came and looked at her.

"Even Teeney notices it," Pam said. "She

282

sits there and looks sorry for me. Don't you, Teeney?"

Martini said, "Yah." She repeated it.

"Scolding me," Pam said. "Thinking, how did I ever get mixed up with a human like that? Ashamed of me."

Jerry gave her a drink. Dorian said, "There, there, Pam. There, there."

The doorbell rang. They let Bill Weigand in. He looked tired. He also looked contented. Given a drink, he looked pleased.

"All right," Pam said. "How?"

"How," Bill said. "How, Jerry. How, Dorian." They responded politely, each saying, "How." Pam said, "You three!" And then she said, "You might have got Mr. Carr shot. I suppose you planned that?"

"She's cross," Jerry said. "She thought it was going to be Miss Barnscott."

Bill nodded. He said, "No, I didn't plan to get Mr. Carr shot. But then — he didn't get shot, of course." He gently removed Sherry from a chair and sat in it. She had made the chair very warm.

"You forgot it was a stag party," Bill said. "That was where you went wrong, Pam."

"A — " Pam said and then, suddenly, she tapped her forehead with two clenched fists. "I'll never live it down," she said. "Not inside. Of *course* it was a stag party."

"Look," Jerry North said to Dorian Weigand, "have you any idea what they're talking about?"

She shook her head.

"It's Braithwaite," Pam said, and appeared to be restored. "It's numbing. Does he admit it, Bill?"

Strothers admitted nothing. It was not to be assumed he would. Thanks to the evidence of two detectives, who had been attentive witnesses, in their seats behind Sam Wyatt, it was not necessary that he should. At least, the assistant district attorney for homicide hoped it would not.

"He had the gun in his pocket," Bill said. "Took it out and fired, not as if he planned to hit anyone. He'd got beyond trying to save the play, I suppose. Wanted to save his skin. After he fired, he grabbed Wyatt, who had started to get up, and struggled with him, pretending to wrestle for the automatic. He was confident we'd believe his version, not Wyatt's. It might have worked, if we hadn't been sure enough already."

"It was all just to stir up the animals?" Dorian said. "The whole thing about Miss Shaw and her going to Chile?"

"Yes," Bill said. "I hoped he'd move. I didn't expect precisely what I got, although I did warn Carr to be ready to dodge. And promised we'd cover him."

"You didn't," Pam said.

"If Strothers had been closer, we would have. At that distance, with an automatic — there isn't one man in a hundred can hit what he aims at. And Strothers didn't aim. That wasn't the idea. The idea was to clinch it against Wyatt. That had more or less been the idea for some time."

He seemed to consider the matter closed. He partly emptied his glass. They looked at him, somewhat coldly. He smiled at them, and said he would spell it out.

"Like C-A-T for cat," Pam said. "Do that."

"Not the whole thing about Miss Shaw and Chile," Bill said. "To stir up the animals, I mean. She and Carr are married. He is going to Chile — not tomorrow, but in about a week. But she isn't going with him. When I left the theater, she was telling Goetz about a new piece of business she wanted in the second act. She's quite an actress."

"You wrote the scene," Dorian told him.

"Not the lines," Bill said. "I suggested an outline. She filled it in."

"Anyway," Pam said, "I knew it wasn't really a kidnapping. Because kidnappers don't carol at their work. I suppose you knew that all the time, too?"

Bill shook his head. The "kidnapping" had,

for a time, presented an obstacle — a piece he could not fit. But then he remembered that the man, according to Naomi's maid, had shouted that Naomi couldn't "get away with it." Bill remembered he had heard Carr use almost that phrase but saying "away from it" — meaning that Naomi could not get away from what they shared.

"L-O-V-E for love," Pam said. "It took them long enough to find it out. But they didn't plan to have it look like a kidnapping?"

They had not, Bill said. They had forgotten, in their excitement — Carr had courted very vigorously — that the maid might overhear. The plan, when they had shouted themselves to agreement, had been merely to slip away, remarry, and tell nobody, since there would have been criticism of a marriage so soon after Fitch's death.

"I should think so," Dorian said.

"Well," Pam said, "probably she forgot she really loved Carr, who was in Pakistan anyway. And thought she loved Fitch."

"And," Jerry said, "all that pretty, pretty money, darlings."

When they were through, Bill said, with patience. She had, at any rate, married Carr. The plan had been to keep it secret until he returned from Chile, then to announce that they had just been remarried. Nellie Blythe's sharp ears had spoiled that. They had returned, to explain that kidnapping was not involved. They had agreed to play the scene as Bill suggested.

"Don't tell me she didn't love it," Pam said.

Bill promised he would not tell her that.

"Sometime," Dorian said, "I wish people would begin at the beginning. Strothers killed Fitch so that Naomi wouldn't marry him and leave the play. He fed him oxalic acid — oh. The stag party. Of *course!*"

Jerry North looked at her. He shook his head slowly, sadly. "I guess it *is* Braithwaite," he said.

"Right," Bill said. Even before the murder, Strothers had started the frame-up against Wyatt which was to cover it. He had suggested that Wyatt arrange to see Fitch, have one more try at changing Fitch's mind. The arrangement, for eleven-thirty, the next morning, had been made at the Friday night party, in Strothers' presence. When he finally admitted going to see Fitch, Wyatt had said that "we" had thought of new arguments, and that Fitch had agreed to listen. But Strothers knew him well, was certain he would only listen, not agree. So Strothers killed him. Strothers had not, of course, been able to anticipate that Wyatt would at first deny having been in Fitch's upstairs rooms. That Wyatt had was, from Strothers' point of view, merely good fortune. But, even without Wyatt's lie, Strothers had provided him as a suspect.

Mrs. Hemmins' discovery of the wadded tea-towel, her identification of it as characteristic of Strothers' habits — "we already knew he was in Fitch's apartment a lot" — had not been fortunate for Strothers. Presumably, she had tried to blackmail him; they had no way of knowing, since Strothers did not talk. Possibly, she had merely been giving him a chance to explain before she went to the police. In any case, he had killed her, and the cat Toby.

"To make it look like Mr. Wyatt, of course," Pam said. "Although it didn't, really. Why didn't he take the tea-towel?"

Presumably, Bill said, because with Mrs. Hemmins dead, he thought it meant nothing — nothing, at any rate, which pointed at him. Also, to get the towel, Strothers would have had to risk getting blood on his shoes, perhaps on his clothing. Getting it had not been worth that chance.

"Also," Bill said, "in case we might be getting ideas, he went to a good deal of trouble when I was at his apartment to spread a tea-towel out smoothly on a rod. Only — he went to too much trouble. Overplayed the scene. Because — the tea-towel wasn't damp, didn't

288

need to be spread to dry. Otherwise, he played the scene very well. His explanation of his visit to Mrs. Hemmins was entirely reasonable. Volunteered, too, which is supposed to be disarming. Also — he had seen Wyatt, who kept blundering in where he would do Strothers the most good — and realized Wyatt might have seen him."

Bill Weigand finished his drink. He raised his eyebrows at Dorian.

"I suppose we'd better," Dorian said. "Get down, Gin."

Gin looked up from Dorian's lap to Dorian's face. Gin purred loudly, as if in entreaty.

"All right," Jerry North said. "I'll ask nicely. I'll say please. The stag party?"

They looked at him in surprise. Bill Weigand was gentle with an old friend, whose mind was numbed by Braithwaite.

"Oxalic acid," Bill said, "has a very bitter taste, which is one reason it is almost never used in homicide. The taste is easy to detect, and since a comparatively large quantity is necessary to kill quickly, the taste has to be disguised. But hangover remedies — some of the more drastic, anyway — will disguise the taste of anything. Right?"

"Yes, teacher," Jerry said.

"So Fitch was killed by someone who knew he had hangovers. And — knew he would have on Saturday morning. Right?"

"Oh," Jerry said.

"His hangover resulted from the party the night before. It was a stag party, so only a man would know Fitch had drunk too much at it. Wyatt left the party early, and Fitch was reasonably sober when Wyatt left. Strothers admitted that himself, presumably because he knew he couldn't get away with denying it. And — Strothers admitted he himself had stayed late, because he couldn't get away with denying that, either. So, he knew Fitch was drunk at the end. So — "

"All right," Jerry North said. "I suppose there were others who stayed late, but all right."

"Several," Bill said. "But, nobody who saw the success he had been working for for years wiped out by Miss Shaw's marriage. Nobody who lived in a third-floor walk-up in a rundown building in the wrong part of the Village. Nobody — "

"All right," Jerry said. "I said all right." The Weigands did not, on close inspection, look like people about to depart. Jerry mixed another round of drinks.

But they must, Pam said, be very careful not to drink too much, even to celebrate. Because hangovers are so dangerous.